The River Leith

ISBN: 978-1626227217
Digital ISBN: 978-1626227200

Cover design Copyright © 2014 by Dar Albert at Wicked Smart Designs
www.wickedsmartdesigns.com

Editing by Keira Andrews
keiraandrews.com

Other Books by Leta Blake

Training Season

Free Read
Stalking Dreams

Tempting Tales with Keira Andrews
Earthly Desires
Ascending Hearts
Love's Nest

"Give me the waters of Lethe that numb the heart, if they exist,
I will still not have the power to forget you."

— Ovid, *The Poems of Exile: Tristia and the Black Sea Letters*

Prologue

Memory, as it turned out, was both everything and nothing. It had no substance, no form, no weight, and no color. It was described, in technical terms, as deposits of proteins within cells of the brain. However, these were words that at their heart were as mysterious and ultimately magical as any other metaphor used in an attempt to understand the concept: memory as a storehouse or set of books—a way to keep track of life's checks and balances; or memory as meaning—a mode of life, and a way of being.

Leith knew now that all these metaphors and all these words boiled down to one thing: memory is the sum of us, the total, and if it is divided, then we are lost.

There were other people in the occupational therapy ward, and Leith studied them with a mixture of horror and envy. There was the droopy, sagging stroke victim Jan Troxell, who could tell anyone the weather report from that morning, but couldn't remember anything else—not her daughter's name, not her age, and not her favorite color.

There was David Mueller, for whom every day began as April 12, 2006, until he found out again, and again, and again that he had suffered a brain injury and couldn't make any more memories.

In some ways these people repulsed Leith, leaving him breathless with terror and disgust at how close he'd come to joining their ranks. People who were shells of the beings they were before, empty and unable to give anything back to the world except for the memory that once they were more, and that they never would be again.

But in other equally scary ways, Leith watched these people

with envy. They were free, utterly rudderless in a thrashing ocean, but still free. Their options had been removed from them, and they were at the mercy of the elements and the grace of people's kindness. But they weren't tied down to memories of who they were, of what and who they'd loved, the things they'd once dreamed, and the things they'd valued.

Leith was not free. He knew who he was, give or take the last three years of his life. It had been almost two weeks since he'd come out of the coma. The illegal blow to the back of his head during the New York Amateur Boxing Championship match had cost his opponent his career, but it had cost Leith a hell of a lot more than that.

All in all he had a lot more than the other amnesiacs he saw every day in the rehab hospital. His intelligence hadn't been compromised, and while some of his motor skills were rough, the doctors told him there was no reason to believe he wouldn't be able to live a completely normal life again. Of course they strongly advised against boxing. Multiple head injuries could be fatal. At least he'd come out of the last one with his life, his brains, and only a few missing years.

His last memory was learning that he would soon be released from prison. In his sparse, clean cell, he'd sat on a bunk and composed a letter to Arthur asking if it would be all right to start over in Brooklyn instead of going home to New Jersey and their father.

Leith had no memory of finishing that letter. No memory of a bus trip from the jail in Florida to Arthur's apartment in Manhattan. No memory of meeting a girl named Naomi on the ski slopes of Vermont. No memory of his father's death and no memory of mourning by his dad's grave. Leith only knew of these things because he'd been told. And he still didn't know how to believe them.

Chapter One

Leith opened his eyes to find his brother Arthur standing in the door to his rehab room with his roguish, floppy blond hair hanging over his forehead and eyes.

"Good afternoon." Arthur flicked his hair back and sat down on the side of the bed, his fashionable and expensive-looking dress shirt tight enough to show off his lithe muscles. Over his arm he held his leather jacket, and on his long, sharp face he wore his usual look of worried appraisal.

"Are we British all of a sudden? Why so formal?"

"Just feeling solemn, baby brother. You of all people know how the moods hit sometimes."

Leith rolled his eyes. Arthur was always a changeable son of a bitch, though to be fair, not half as mercurial as Leith. It was yet another way Arthur had always been somehow less than Leith. The only thing Arthur had more of, in Leith's own estimation, was brains. Otherwise he was less handsome, less athletic, less impulsive, and less moody.

Since he was six years older than Leith, Arthur should have been by all rights larger, yet he was shaped like a whip while Leith had always been a hammer. Leith still couldn't believe he was twenty-three, and Arthur twenty-nine. Almost *thirty*!

Arthur had always been there for him, and Leith loved him more than he liked to say. As an unexpected pang of emotion waved through him, he almost made a familiar joke about his brother's lack of physical substance, but he wasn't looking so strong and healthy himself these days. A month in a bed would do that to a body.

He'd once been six feet of pure muscle, but now he was soft

and weak. The nurses assured him he'd soon be fit enough once he was cleared for exercise. A certain impertinent nurse with red hair and an upturned nose had also claimed he was still the handsomest patient on the unit. Given what he knew of the rest of the patients, Leith understood it was more of a tease than a true compliment, but his vanity clung to it anyway.

With his full lips, long eyelashes, and the golden flecks in his hazel eyes, he'd always thought he was a pretty good looking guy, and he was pleased a little brain trauma hadn't changed *that*, at least.

Leith licked his dry lips, and seeing Arthur's empty hands decided to get in a dig of another kind. "Gee, thanks for bringing your little bro something decent to eat. It's not like I'm starving to death in here or anything."

"Sorry. Not today. But don't worry—you won't go hungry."

"Speak for yourself. You know what the food here is like."

Arthur ignored his bitching and reached out to smooth Leith's light brown hair. "We need to get you a haircut."

"What? I look great."

"Sure, you're sexy as a devil." Arthur brushed at Leith's clothes like he was dusting him off, and then said, "Leith, listen up. There's someone here to see you, and you need to be incredibly kind to him."

"Okay. Why? What's wrong with him?"

"Nothing's wrong with him. He's just been worried for you. We'll talk about the specifics later, but for now…let him hug you and touch you, okay? Let him have a little reassurance. He needs that now."

Leith frowned. "Is this a friend of mine?"

"Yes. He's your best friend. His name is Zachariah Stephens. Does that sound familiar? You call him Zach."

"Zach?" Leith said the name a few times, trying out both the long and short versions. "I don't remember. He's my best friend?" Leith hadn't had someone he would have called a best friend since childhood. And even then it'd been Arthur. Did grown men even declare friendships like that? It seemed a little weird.

But Leith didn't question it because the end of Arthur's nose went red, and his gray eyes swam as they always did when Leith didn't remember something or someone important. "He's the best friend you've ever had. Be nice to him." Arthur patted his arm as he stood. "Let him hug you."

Leith took a deep breath and sat up straighter in his bed. So far he'd met a black girl with an afro named Marian, and a blonde big-boobed girl with a nice laugh called Ava. He understood that he lived in a walk-up in Park Slope with Marian and Ava, but he didn't remember anything about them, not even when they told him stories about how they became friends, things they'd done together, and places they'd been.

He could tell they'd all been worried—disturbed even by how blankly he looked at them. So he was determined to do better for this Zach, his best friend. He attempted a pleasant expression and waited patiently.

Arthur looked at him one last time before opening the door and saying to whoever was waiting outside, "Okay, he's ready for you."

Leith smiled at the handsome and trim black-haired guy in dark trendy jeans and a bright green T-shirt as he came into the room, feeling suddenly aware of his own pajama bottoms and t-shirt. This Zachariah held a basket and wore a very tentative expression.

"Hello, Leith," he said, his smile tremulous and full of bravado.

He looked about five years older than Leith, and about four

inches shorter. His limbs were long and lanky, and his hips were quite narrow, which somehow made him seem smaller than he really was. He had lush lips and pale skin. From behind the stranger, Arthur nodded a goodbye, mouthing the words, "Hug him," again.

Leith searched for any kind of memory of this man, his supposed "best friend." *Nada. Nip. Nothing.* He kept smiling even though he may as well have never seen him before in his life.

The guy cleared his throat, his expression full of worry, and he glanced over his shoulder at the door Arthur had just closed behind him.

Leith charged ahead into the moment. What choice did he have really? Unless something changed, this was going to be his life for a while. "Hi…Zach?"

Zach's head snapped forward. His eyes sparked, and he took a sharp breath. "You—?"

Leith shook his head, sorry that he'd blown it already by giving his friend false hope. "That's your name, right? Zachariah…something. Smith? No, Stephens, right? I'm sorry. Arthur told me."

"Oh right. Of course. I expected that, but I guess I'd hoped…" Zach's smile didn't crinkle his eyes, and he looked as though he'd taken a hit to the gut.

Leith tried to appear sympathetic. "I'm sorry I don't remember you, but Arthur says that we're good friends? If that's the case, I'm sure I'll like you again…when I get to know you. Again."

It was awkward dealing with people who had emotional attachments to him that he didn't know how to return. He wasn't even sure if what he said was true. He assumed it was, because he'd generally picked good friends in the past. Why this guy was so special—why he warranted the title "best"—Leith didn't know, but if he'd given it to him once, then surely Zach would earn it again.

Zach's eyes drew Leith's attention. He studied them, trying to decide if they were green or blue, or something in between. But the color was only part of it; he didn't look away because there was something in Zach's eyes that made his throat ache.

Suddenly he remembered being twelve years old, playing in a field behind the house and stumbling across a green and yellow bird, a golden-crowned kinglet, sitting motionless in the grass. It was beautiful, and delicate, and broken. Its wing was twisted out from its side, and Leith's heart had ached when the beautiful bird fluttered into a screeching and pained flight into a nearby bush, hiding itself from him.

"So," Leith said, swallowing hard and releasing the memory of the bird. "Um, how have you been?"

Zach ignored the question and held up the basket. "I brought your favorite."

"Oh yeah? Give it here." Leith made grabby hands, hoping that a show of friendly charm would make the moment less tense. "What's in it?"

"Food," Zach said. "As I recall, you're quite fond of it."

Leith noticed his soft, Southern accent. A small burble of laughter began in Leith's chest, and his mouth relaxed into a natural smile. "A big fan," he agreed, indicating again that Zach should give him the basket immediately.

Zach drew closer to the bed, dropped it next to Leith's leg, and then stood to the side, one arm over his chest and the other hanging down. Leith could feel Zach's eyes on him as he flipped back the napkin covering the food. Zach's gaze made Leith think of the time when his mother had been in the hospital right before her death. He'd stood by her bed, afraid to leave her side, trying to memorize everything about her.

"This looks amazing." Leith lifted up a loaf of sweet Easter bread. "My favorite! I haven't had this in *years*. My mother used to make this every…" Leith trailed off and glanced at Zach, who was nodding very slowly, his face blank in a way that seemed intentional, his eyes focused on the bread. "Did you make this?"

Zach's mouth twitched, and he drew closer to the bed, leaning his thighs against the edge of it. The tips of his fingers rested on the mattress next to Leith's leg. "No, I'm not much of a baker. Ava made it."

Leith took the information in with the feeling of resignation that was becoming his daily norm. "Ah, so Ava remembered that I liked it. That's sweet. Thank her for me."

Zach shifted slightly, and his movement alerted Leith that he must have said something unkind without even knowing it. "I'm sorry?" Leith said again, lost and worried, looking up into Zach's eyes, which were shining with feelings that Leith couldn't begin to sift through.

"Don't be ridiculous. I don't know what you're sorry for," Zach said, forcing a smile. "There are other things you like in there too. Dates, Turkish figs, and that cheese you once told me you'd marry if it was legal."

"Is it Swiss?"

Zach shook his head, seeming to vibrate with anxiety. "You buy it at Grand Army Plaza Greenmarket usually. Do you remember that?"

"Yeah." He'd gone there with Arthur when he'd visited Park Slope as a teen, before…well, before everything, actually.

"You'd buy it and get some fresh bread from Daggi. She's a little old German lady that flirts with you. And here are some fresh blueberries for the yogurt—"

"Zach?" Leith interrupted.

"Yes?" Zach's voice was breathless and edgy.

There was something he should say or do, and it was right

there just out of his reach. It was something to do with the bread, and something to do with the way Zach had moved back ever so slightly. "Did you ask Ava to make the bread because *you* knew I liked it?"

Zach smiled. "Sure, I know you like all these things."

It was a nice enough smile, but somehow Leith knew it wasn't the real thing. "Well, then…thank you."

"If there's anything else you'd want—"

"No. This is good. This is amazing. I'll have it all eaten—"

"By noon."

"Probably," Leith agreed, tearing into the bread. It was good—exactly the way his mother's had tasted. He chewed slowly and then reached for the water he kept by the bed. Leith swallowed and pointed toward the soft fold-out chair in the corner, the one that Arthur had slept in for a few nights when they first moved him to this facility. "Pull it up and have a seat. We'll talk."

Zach seemed to consider this for a moment, and Leith wondered if his friend was simply so uncomfortable with the situation that he was going to leave. Instead, Zach pulled the chair over very close and perched on the edge of it. He closed his eyes, and took some slow deep breaths. When he opened his eyes again he looked much more relaxed.

"That's better," Leith said.

Zach let out an even deeper breath. "By the way, Marian asked me to tell you hello."

"You know Marian?"

Zach nodded, his eyes on his hands. "I live in the apartment."

"Our apartment? With me and Marian? And that girl, um, Ava?"

"Yes."

"Why didn't anyone mention it before?"

Zach shrugged. "The doctors thought we shouldn't rush you by all of us swarming in right from the beginning. Besides, they said you might remember on your own in time."

"Time." Leith sighed. "I feel like all I hear about now is time. 'Give it time.' 'Have some patience.' 'In time.' It's endless."

"Time is just about the only thing I want to think about right now, honestly," Zach said, sinking into the chair.

Leith really had no idea what Zach meant, and he didn't get the impression that Zach wanted to clarify. Leith took another drink of water, and waved the bottle toward Zach in an unspoken offer. After shaking his head, Zach relaxed into the chair, resting his head against the back. The angle emphasized the dark circles under Zach's eyes.

"You seem pretty tired," Leith said. "What do you do for work?"

"Oh, it's not my work. I've just had a hard time sleeping lately."

Leith let that response sink in. "It's hard to sleep here too. Someone is always checking in on you or stabbing you with something sharp."

Zach's face softened with a smile.

"There, you're relaxing now," Leith said, taking another bite of bread. "When you came in, you reminded me of this bird when I was a kid, a hurt bird, right before he took off flying."

Zach's eyes flashed. "Leith, I'm not going anywhere."

Leith stopped chewing his food. The intensity of Zach's voice was unexpected, sudden, and full of something that made Leith's stomach clench and his breath draw in sharply. He drank some more water, washing it away.

He tried to think of something to say that wouldn't upset Zach. "So, how did I meet you?"

Sitting up straight, Zach said with false lightness, "I was on a cruise ship—"

"We met on a cruise ship?"

"No." He laughed.

It was a really nice sound that made Leith feel warm and calm.

"I worked on a cruise ship as a steward for five years. When I decided to settle in one place and stay for good, my sister suggested I come to New York and move in with her." He chuckled again. "Well, let's just say that we're great siblings but terrible roommates. That didn't last long. Once I had a steady job, I started looking for a new place to stay. You and the girls were renting out the den as a bedroom. I answered your ad."

"This was before my father died?"

"No, it was a while after that."

Leith looked down at his hands. He hated thinking of his father's death. He felt impotent, and angry, and most of all like he'd drown in a river of regrets if he let himself really feel it. "I went to stay with Arthur in Brooklyn instead of going home to my dad when I got out of prison," Leith said, trying to understand it again. "I wasn't there for him."

"Leith," Zach said, his voice smooth and calm. "Your father knew how much you loved him."

Making a soft sound, Leith shook his head. "Yeah. You're probably right." But he wasn't sure at all. "Do you...did I tell you why I was in prison?" It was years ago to everyone else, but he still expected to wake in his cell with old Hal snoring in the bunk above.

"A third degree felony. You were involved in an illegal underground MMA fight with unfortunate consequences." Zach's expression remained neutral.

It was strange how clearly he remembered *that* night—the

15

make-shift cage, the adrenaline rush, the fear, and the blood—but he couldn't remember the entirely legal boxing match that had landed him here.

"I know I'm right. Your father knew you loved him."

Leith's chest tightened. "How?"

"Because you told me the two of you made up before he died."

"We did?"

Zach nodded.

Leith's throat tightened and he stared down into the basket of food, trying to get control. He just wished he could have seen his father one last time. Though from what Zach said, perhaps he had. Maybe a picture would help.

"Zach," Leith said, turning and looking him in the eye. "You asked if there was anything else you could bring me."

"Yes." Zach leaned forward. "Anything."

"Can you bring some photos?"

"Of your father?"

"Yes, and some from my life these last three years or so? I got a card from a girl. Naomi? An ex-girlfriend, Arthur said. I don't even know what she looks like. Maybe if I saw her picture..."

Zach pressed his lips together and nodded slowly, his eyes flickering. "Sure. I'll bring them tomorrow."

Zach's eyes made Leith think again of the kinglet's wings as they'd shimmered in the sunlight. "Thanks." The air in the room felt heavy. He grabbed the item on top of the basket, keeping his tone light. "This is the cheese I want to marry, huh?"

Standing up, Zach clapped his hands lightly in an almost effeminate manner, and the sound broke the moment. The question seemed to bring about a change in Zach, who said, "Yes, it's your true love. Or so you declared to me a few months ago."

Zach's eyes smiled, filled with amused affection. Leith liked it. He wondered what he could say to make Zach smile like that again. It looked much better on him than the tense sadness he'd come in wearing. Then, just as suddenly, the smile was gone.

"I guess I should leave now."

Leith's surprise must have shown on his face. "But you just got here." *And I was just starting to feel comfortable with you.*

"I wish I could stay, but I…really can't."

"You don't want to share this cheese?"

"Polyamory was never your style," Zach countered, and then smiled warmly again.

His teeth were very white, and his lips a reddish pink. Leith thought Zach came across as a little prissy, a little uptight, but something about it made him feel like laughing inside. He must have found him amusing before. Obviously, or else they wouldn't be *best friends.*

"The thing is, I have a business to run," Zach went on. "Unfortunately I need to go."

"What kind of business?"

"A bar."

"Oh, my brother owns a bar. On Fifth Avenue in Park Slope. Or so he tells me. Supposedly I used to work—" Leith let the sentence hang. "Right, so you know that, don't you?"

Zach spun around, moving the chair back into its original position. But Leith had seen his face twist like he was fighting tears.

He faced Leith again. "Believe it or not it's the same bar. Arthur's my business partner. I'll tell you all about it another day, okay? The doctors say it's time to start introducing you to some of your history, now that you've dealt with—" Zach stopped short.

"My father's death?"

"It takes some time."

"Time!" Leith said, and threw his hands up.

"Yes." Zach stiffly lifted his right hand in a flat-palmed wave. "Well, see you."

"When? Tomorrow?"

Zach nodded, smiling softly. "Sure, if you want."

"You'll bring pictures?"

"Sure." Zach stood there a long moment, and then turned.

Leith noticed there were multiple decorative zippers on the back pockets of Zach's jeans, drawing attention to his ass. When Zach looked back at the door, Leith jerked his head up.

"All right then. Goodbye." Zach's voice was tight, and he seemed as tense as he'd been when he came in.

Leith remembered what Arthur had said, and he called out just as Zach's hand touched the door knob. "Zach?"

When Zach turned, his eyes were a hot green, and his lips trembled a little. "Yes?"

"Hey, uh, before you leave…?" Leith held out his arm to indicate the offer of a hug.

Zach hesitated, lower lip in his teeth, but then crossed over to Leith solemnly. When Zach bent down to hug him, Leith felt him relax in his arms. Leith closed his eyes, surprised when his left hand cupped the back of Zach's neck in an unplanned motion, his fingers tracing the soft hair there. He took a deep breath. A sweet, spicy scent filled his lungs, and suddenly he was warm all over. His heart jolted. He'd smelled that before. Somewhere. He took another deep breath.

"Don't forget—I'm not going anywhere," Zach whispered fiercely.

"I thought you were going to work," Leith whispered, turning his face toward Zach's ear, having an odd urge to taste the cologne he smelled.

Zach pulled away, his eyes laughing. "You always think you're so funny, don't you?"

For a moment Leith thought something else was about to happen, something that made him lick his lips and hold his breath. But then it passed, and he felt like he'd missed something important.

Zach grabbed a piece of the bread. "You don't mind sharing?"

Leith was tempted to grab it back, thinking that somehow that would be the right thing to do, but he simply shrugged.

"See you tomorrow, Leith."

"See you." Leith said, watching the door shut behind Zach. He smelled his fingers. The sweet-spicy scent of Zach's cologne clung to them, and deep inside his brain something stirred. It made him jumpy; like there was an itch in there he simply couldn't scratch.

ONE MONTH EARLIER
VLOG ENTRY #1

INT. BAR – BOOTH – NIGHT
Zach adjusts the camera on his laptop and leans back. He smiles and salutes.

ZACH
Greetings, friends, Romans, and countrymen! Lend me your ears! Yes, I know, I know. Long time no see, huh? Can you believe it's been three whole years since I stopped vlogging about my thrilling life on a cruise ship and started vlogging about my boring life in Brooklyn? Plenty of you hung on with me through that transition, and I appreciated that loyalty. And how did I repay you? I disappeared for the past year! Sure, things here have been incredibly busy, but that's no excuse for neglecting you, my loyal followers.

So, I'm here to catch you up on all the latest excitement going on in my new life here in the Big Apple! First...

He stretches his arms wide, indicating the booth he's seated in, and the blue and green décor behind him.

My bar! Blue Flight! Yes, you heard it right. I, Zachariah Stephens, am officially part owner of this fine, and if I say so myself, cooler-than-cool establishment. Can you believe it? Everyone who's known me my whole life can tell you that I've wanted to own a bar since I was five years old and swirled my first fake martini in a doll's tea cup.

Blue Flight is an absolute dream come true. Oh, and get this—our apartment is just above it. I barely roll out of bed and I'm at work in the morning. My commute is a staircase. Envy me.

And it's all thanks to my wonderful, amazing, and beautiful sister, Maddie, who provided me with a serious cash infusion in the form of a big, fat loan, making all of this...

He indicates the room again.

...possible! And, Maddie, if you ever see this, *mwah*! You're the best! Thank you, thank you! I forgive you for outing me to Mom when I was twelve! All is forgiven!

Zach's smile fades, and his gaze moves away from the camera.

And then there's Leith. I've told you about him before, back when we started our unexpected little romance. Well, Leith has a championship boxing match tomorrow. It's the most important title bout of his career. I'm excited for him, and I know he's worked up too. But lately we seem to get into small fights over every little thing.

He crosses his arms over his chest.

Of course, Leith is anxious. Very anxious. And saying that he deals well with anxiety is like saying that I'm a virgin. So right now everything I do or say annoys him, and my attempts to help him are seen as nuisances rather than as the

21

acts of kindness, support, and love they're intended to be. I don't know what to do for him when he gets like this. He can be such an ass.

He sighs and gathers himself.

Ah well, it doesn't really matter. Leith knows that I love him, and that I want only good things for him, and I know that he loves me. Now all he has to do is defeat this meathead in the ring, and then things will go back to normal. When it comes to knocking out 160 pounds of muscle in the boxing ring, he's a champion. When it comes to dealing with anxiety, he's a bull in a china shop.

Zach shrugs and leans forward.

If this is the price I occasionally have to pay for the happiness our life together brings me, then it's more than worth it. Most of the time, we're the perfect couple, and we fit together brilliantly. If I weren't part of us, I'd envy us. We are *that* good—

LEITH (*off screen*)
Zach?

ZACH
Here!

LEITH
There you are. Are you talking to yourself? Should I be worried?

Leith leans into the booth and kisses Zach, cupping his hand on the back of Zach's neck.

I couldn't sleep. I kept thinking about how grumpy I was with you earlier. I'm sorry. I'm an ass.

ZACH

Okay.

LEITH

Okay? "Okay" you agree that I'm an ass?

ZACH

Yep. Absolutely. Of course, it takes one to know one. But, hey, scoot over here so the camera can get a good picture of your pretty face.

Zach moves over and Leith slides in close to him in the booth.

I've started up my YouTube channel again. I'm making a video blog about all the amazing things that have happened in the last year. Well, and about how you, Mr. Wenz, are sometimes a giant ass.

LEITH

And you're doing it *now*? It's almost midnight.

ZACH

It's a good distraction from what an ass my boyfriend is being.

LEITH

Are you really filming right now? I'm wearing my pajamas.

ZACH

Boxers and a T-shirt. Oh yes, the viewers will be scandalized.

LEITH

Seriously Zach, I'm really sorry about earlier. I shouldn't be such a dick to you. I know you're just trying to help, and I appreciate it. I do.

ZACH

He turns to the camera, keeping his arm around Leith's neck and shaking him a little.

See, my loves? He's much too pretty and sweet to stay angry with for long.

LEITH

You've really been telling them about our fight?

ZACH

Don't worry. You didn't come off too badly. I'd already moved on to telling them that, truly, we're the perfect couple.

LEITH

He looks straight at the camera.

Well, I don't know about that, but it's true that my boyfriend here likes to brag.

ZACH

I only tell the truth. They'll just have to suffer the same soul-crushing envy that everyone else who knows us suffers from.

Leith scoffs as Zach chuckles and kisses him again. Leith cups his face and tilts his head, deepening the kiss. Zach breaks away.

ZACH

Okay, perhaps we should wrap this up. It's only eight hours until my sweetie here has to be up and at 'em to prepare for his boxing match.

LEITH

Seven.

ZACH

Seven? It's later than I thought. We need to get your fuzzy head to bed. So, my loves—I'll see you tomorrow! Or rather, you'll see me!

LEITH

Tomorrow? You're going to make this a regular thing?

ZACH

Yeah. It's fun, and it's good for me to get things off of my chest, don't you think?

LEITH

Sure. Comment below if you think Zach is a dork.

He avoids Zach's attempt to smack the back of his head.

ZACH

Until tomorrow! *Mwah*!

LEITH

Adios, Zach's amigos.

Chapter Two

The hospital garden was in full summer bloom. The roses were especially lush and vibrant, appearing ready to burst with delicious-smelling beauty. His psychiatrist, Dr. Thakur, suggested they take a walk together during their session to help Leith get some strength back. As they strolled, Leith was vaguely embarrassed that his stamina wasn't even half as good his doctor's. He had to pause and catch his breath more than once.

As he did, Leith took the opportunity to study Dr. Thakur's now familiar laugh lines around his twinkling dark brown eyes, his smooth dark skin, and his pitch-black hair. He was slightly rotund, and that, along with his age, reminded Leith of his father.

But that was where the resemblance ended. Leith's father had been fully German—with blond hair and blue eyes—and an alcoholic gambling addict, while Dr. Thakur was a successful, self-contained man who didn't seem likely to bet on anything.

"I've been checking in with the physical therapists," Dr. Thakur said in his mild Chicago accent. His strong hand supported Leith's waist when he wavered on the path. "You're making good progress, but we all believe getting outside more will be good for you. As long as the weather holds, I'd like you to walk out here every day."

It wasn't as though Leith had been confined to his room since he'd been moved to the rehabilitation facility. He was allowed free reign of the premises for the most part, so long as he alerted the nurses to his destination, but usually he didn't go as far as the gardens. There were plenty of pretty nurses to talk to until he grew tired, and Leith would generally leave his flirtations to go back to his room well before he made it all the way to the door to the outside world.

But now he wondered why he hadn't had more fortitude. Damn, it was good to see the blue sky and white clouds above. Leith always breathed deeper and easier out in the fresh air.

"How long until I'm released?" He wanted to go camping. Getting out into the woods had healed him as a kid, especially after his mother's death. He wanted to lie back under the stars, and count them into the wee hours of the morning.

Dr. Thakur indicated a bench behind a large shrub and sheltered by an oak tree, and they sat. "Well, that depends. I hear you had a pretty big outburst over a hunk of clay in art therapy this morning."

Leith crossed his arms over his chest and leaned back. He still felt weak from the walk, and he was definitely not interested in talking about his *feelings* again. "Yeah, so what? I was frustrated."

"Obviously."

"I couldn't get it to do what I wanted."

"So you threw it against the wall?"

Leith exhaled sharply and looked away. It was difficult to explain. He'd been staring at the clay and thinking about Zach for some reason. Thinking about the sweet Easter bread, and how, had the clay been a slightly different color, it would have looked a lot like the yeasty, thick dough that his mother had made. Then he'd thought about Zach's eyes, and the memory of that small bird had come to him again.

Using the tongue depressors they'd handed out as molding tools, he'd tried to make the bird he saw in his mind's eye. When the delicate wing he'd carefully scraped out of the hunk of clay suddenly buckled and broke, an avalanche released inside of him, and moments later he'd been brought down to the floor by several male nurses. He remembered throwing the clay, and he remembered turning over the table, but he didn't know exactly why he'd reacted that way.

"I was angry," Leith said, feeling sheepish. He didn't meet his doctor's eyes.

"Leith, we know that you want to leave rehabilitation. You've already made remarkable physical progress. Truly, we'd like you to be ready as well, but so long as you're still having a difficult time managing your anger, it would be irresponsible for me to release you. Believe me, the outside world is going to be a lot harder for you to negotiate than an art therapy class."

Leith exhaled, and just shook his head.

"The expectations and hopes of your friends and family are difficult enough for you to manage now, and you're not with them every day. Before we give you the go-ahead, I want you to be more comfortable with the people you'll be living with. We don't want another episode like today, or worse, like the first one."

Leith closed his eyes, shuddering as he remembered. He'd just woken up, and though he later learned it wasn't for the first time, it was the first time he could recall, and the first time he was coherent and able to speak. Arthur had been sitting by his hospital bed, looking thinner than ever and worn completely through.

"What happened?" Leith had asked, a sensation like bees buzzing rose up through his body as he looked around the room. "Where am I?" It didn't look like the prison infirmary.

"You're in the hospital," Arthur answered. His voice was full of quiet affection, and he'd sat even closer, taking Leith's hand in his own. "You should stay calm. I'll get a nurse."

"What happened?" Leith asked again.

Arthur had shook his head, and closed his eyes a moment, as though wishing it away. "There was a...mishap. In the ring."

Leith didn't understand. What ring? A mishap? He had a million questions, but the words were jammed up. He didn't feel right. Something was off, and he wasn't sure what it was, but he was wound tight, like a spring about to let loose. What was Arthur doing in Florida? It had to be bad for him to come all the way from New York. "Am I going to die?"

"No, of course not. You're on the mend now." Arthur had patted Leith's chest, smiled through teary eyes, and then cleared his throat. "Where's my phone? I told him to get some sleep. He'll be upset he's not here. I should call right away—"

Leith had blinked and looked around. If he was in the hospital, and that crazy pounding feeling in his chest was right, and things were definitely not good, their father should definitely be there. "Are you calling Dad?"

Arthur froze with his cell phone in his hand. His eyebrows drew together. "Leith, our father is dead." He'd looked at Leith carefully. "You know that. He's been gone for almost three years. Not long after you came back from prison."

"What? Came back? I'm not out yet!" Leith had started to claw at his arms, trying to get rid of the feeling that he was stuck in his skin as panic rose in him. "Bullshit! Is this your idea of a joke?"

Arthur had backed away from the bed. "Let me get someone. Just a second, Leith. Everything's okay—"

Leith's heart pounded. "Don't lie to me," he'd yelled, ripping the cords and IVs from his arms and chest. Alarms rang, but no guards came. "Why am I here? Where am I? What are you doing to me? Let me out. I want out!"

As nurses burst in, Arthur rushed to hold him back, but Leith lashed out, and the sound of his fist hitting Arthur's jaw had cracked through the room.

Blinking, Leith focused on the fresh-cut grass at his feet. He was wearing ridiculous slippers that should have embarrassed him, but after two years in an orange jumpsuit, pajamas and slippers were a step up. It was still hard to believe he'd been out for three years. Yet here he was, right back in a different kind of prison.

Dr. Thakur waited patiently beside him, and Leith wasn't sure how long it had been since either of them had spoken. "But you said I had a bad reaction to the anti-seizure medication, and my brain was swollen. It's better now, isn't it?"

"Yes, we've adjusted your meds, and the swelling has subsided. But your frontal lobe sustained some damage, and the unconscious psychological trauma of knowing that something was wrong—and being unable to place yourself in the world or in time—is still affecting you. Your extreme fight or flight reaction occurs when you experience emotional stimulus that your over-taxed brain can't handle."

"It was just clay," Leith muttered.

"Until we can at least hope that you'll choose flight over fight if triggered, we must continue to be slow in your introduction to the parts of the past you don't remember."

"I'm just afraid—" Leith began, and then stopped.

"Of?"

"I'm afraid I won't ever remember it."

"And what's so bad about that?" Dr. Thakur asked.

Thinking inexplicably of Zach's face as he'd turned away the day before, fighting tears, Leith said, "I don't want to let anyone down."

"Who are you afraid of letting down?"

Leith shrugged. "People. My friends."

"Like your friend you met yesterday? Zachariah Stephens?"

Leith turned his head and studied the red roses on the other side of the gravel path. "I don't know. A little. It's everyone really."

31

"Do you think it's possibly significant that you had that outburst this morning after meeting him?"

Leith looked back to study Dr. Thakur's face, looking for a clue as to what he was missing. "Why? *Is* it significant? Should I think it is?"

"That's your call. I was simply curious."

Leith shrugged, and they sat in silence as he remembered the moments just before his rage that morning. Quietly, he said, "It isn't just time or memories that I'm missing. I feel like I've lost who I am. Like, there's this feeling that I'm a big, human-shaped lump of clay, and *I'm* somewhere inside it if I could just dig myself out. But I can't *remember* who that person is supposed to be anymore."

Dr. Thakur didn't say anything until Leith looked at him again. Then he spoke with a deep empathy that made Leith feel safe, like a small, well-liked child.

"Leith, a lump of clay could be formed into almost anything by a person with skillful hands. If you remember your past, that might be a blessing, and it might not be. I couldn't possibly judge that. What I know is that you're the artist of your life, and you can mold this hunk of clay into anything you want. You don't have to take anyone else into consideration, unless you want to do so."

Leith thought of the wing he'd been working on in art therapy—the way it had emerged so beautifully from the clay before the failure of his hands had been revealed, and it folded and broke under its own weight. "I'm not much of an artist," he whispered.

Dr. Thakur put his hand on Leith's shoulder and shook him a little. "I think you'll make it just fine. Just watch that you don't throw your life against the wall too."

ꙮ ꙮ ꙮ

Zach didn't come again after all. Instead Marian and Ava showed up with a basket of food and an excuse from Zach—something about a late night. But Marian didn't meet Leith's eyes for the first few minutes after they arrived, which made his stomach hurt for some reason.

"So, what did I used to do in my spare time?" Leith asked them, munching on the fresh grapes from the basket Zach had sent. His eyes occasionally strayed to the tops of Ava's breasts on display in her v-neck sweater. They looked soft and reminded him of his mother's chest, which he'd used as a pillow when he was still a tiny, sleepy child.

Marian shrugged. "Mainly you and Zach would hang out. Sometimes we'd all play foosball or have a movie night, but you kept yourself busy with training."

"What did Zach and I do together?" Leith asked, wondering if they went camping or hiking. For some reason, Zach didn't seem the type.

Ava blinked rapidly for a moment, and caught Marian's gaze. Then she smiled brightly. "You know, stuff. You talked. Joked a lot. That sort of thing. Can I have a grape?"

"Sure," Leith said, passing the fruit to her. He wanted to ask them more about Zach but he didn't know what to say. "Zach seems like a really nice person."

"Yeah," Marian said, stuffing a few grapes in her mouth too. "Super nice."

Leith thought about Zach's smile and his eyes, and the sweet-spicy scent of his cologne. "He's probably got a lot of friends."

"Zach sure never met a stranger," Marian agreed.

"That's what I thought." Leith sighed.

Marian and Ava looked at each other, both of them stuffing more grapes into their mouths. Leith thought Ava in particular looked good with her mouth full, but he was distracted enough by their strange eyebrow-arching exchange that he didn't let his thoughts go too far down that path.

"What?"

Ava chewed quickly, swallowed her mouthful of grapes, and said, "Oh! I just remembered..." She fished around in her purse and pulled out a flat, smooth cell phone. "Yours. Arthur said to give it to you." She stood up and leaned against the bed, pressing the phone on. "See? It's programmed already. From before."

She showed him the various functions, and Leith noted that Zach was the first listed under Favorites, followed by Arthur, and then Marian and Ava. He leaned a little toward her; he could smell her perfume, something light and airy, and it made him feel calm and a little happy. The emotional response to her scent was interesting, mainly because it seemed so mild in comparison to the jolt he'd felt from Zach's cologne.

He considered asking Marian or Ava to bring a sample of Zach's cologne to him, so he could smell it whenever he wanted. It made his mind itchy to even think of the scent, and yet he knew what a strange request that would be. He stayed silent.

Ava said she had to get to work, and kissed him on the cheek. Marian stuck around for a while longer, though Leith didn't really know what to talk to her about. She told him that Ava worked as the manager of an attorney's office, and mentioned someone named LaMarcus.

He wasn't sure who that was, but he tried to feign some interest in the conversation once he discovered it was Marian's little brother. He found that it was easier to pretend to care sometimes than to admit that he simply had no clue about a subject and didn't really want to gain one.

In the afternoon, Leith sat through a group therapy session with David Mueller, who was crying, again, about the fact that he just found out—again—that he couldn't make any more memories. Also Jan Troxell repeating the weather report for the morning, and then bursting into tears because she couldn't remember her daughter's name...again.

Leith always left these sessions feeling depressed and frustrated. He usually offered up a few meager sentences of his own, mostly about his concern that his brother had to spend so much money and time on him, and sometimes he'd mention that he was angry his father had died during the time that he couldn't remember.

But he said as little as possible for so many reasons. For one thing, David Mueller and Jan Troxell wouldn't remember what he said next session anyway. As for the counselor, she was boring and never offered up anything that he didn't already know for himself. "It'll take some time," Leith muttered under his breath along with her.

The rehab facility's food was dry and tasteless, and Leith pitied Arthur almost as much as he pitied himself as he watched his brother choke down a tray of it late that afternoon by Leith's bed.

"Arthur," Leith said, pushing his food around on his plate. "Have you ever smelled something, and it reminded you of something else, but you couldn't think of just what?"

Arthur looked up, his eyes narrowed with curiosity. "Sure, everyone experiences that. What makes you ask? Have you remembered something? Something you'd forgotten?"

Leith thought of the bird again, the small wounded thing that flew into the brush and hid itself from him. He thought of Zach's eyes, and the way he'd looked at Leith, and he shook his head. "No, nothing in particular. There was a bird once, a long time ago. I keep thinking of him. A little golden-crowned kinglet."

Arthur shrugged, and took another bite of his food before

35

pushing the tray away and leaning back in the soft chair. "There were birds all over the old house when we were kids."

"Yeah." Leith shrugged too. "Arthur, what did I do besides boxing? I asked Marian and Ava earlier, but they weren't much help. Didn't I have any hobbies?"

"You went to school and had a job in my bar," Arthur said, smiling and sniffing a little ostentatiously. "It's a nice place. You worked the bar, waited tables, and did a little clean up. It gave you enough income so you could afford your books and school. And your training costs, since you insisted on boxing."

Leith searched his mind. He didn't remember ever being behind a bar, much less working one. Or going to college, for that matter. He'd talked about his plans to go while he was in prison, but last he knew, all he had was a high school diploma and a criminal record. He tried to imagine himself in a lecture hall and failed miserably.

Arthur smiled at him, gray eyes gleaming. "You could come back when you get out. Though you'll have to ask Zach about it, I guess. I'm sure he won't—well, I doubt he'd mind." Arthur sounded suddenly hesitant. "Ah well, we'll have to see how it all turns out. It's hard to say just now. There's so much we have to wait and see about."

"Does the doctor actually think I'll ever get my memory back?" Leith had never asked outright, and no one had ever given him any direct information about this aspect of his prognosis.

Arthur waved a hand as though it were an unimportant consideration. "Why bother worrying about that now? You have a lot on your mind—"

"Arthur," Leith said. "It's my life. I have a right to know these things."

Arthur nodded slowly, and then pushed the chair back a bit. That small motion alone told Leith all he needed to know.

"Well," Arthur began, averting his eyes, and then templing his long fingers in his lap before looking at Leith again. "The doctor believes that, due to the location and extent of your injury, the chances of you regaining your memory are rather slim. We've been told that we can't expect it to happen...ever. And...some of us have had a harder time with that than others."

"Who's us?"

"Your friends and me, of course." Arthur pursed his lips in a cynical way. "The psychiatrist told us that it's a process of grieving. Denial, anger, bargaining, blah blah blah," Arthur waved his hand again. "The main thing is that you're alive, you're here, and you'll be just fine." He gripped Leith's forearm and squeezed it. "Just fine, do you understand?"

Leith nodded, and took a slow breath. He wondered what stage of grief he was in, or if what he felt was grief at all. He pushed the plate of food away and nodded toward the corner of his room where there was a small table. "Hand me that basket. I think there's some of that cheese left. Have you tasted it? Zach said it's my favorite."

Arthur reached the basket to Leith, saying softly, "Zach would know."

⚘ ⚘ ⚘

That night, Leith flicked through the various screens on his cell phone. There were only a few photos on the phone, and no text messages. It was as though it had all been cleared off. Leith looked at the pictures: one of Arthur with his arm around a dark-haired woman wearing a Blue Flight T-shirt, and one of Zach behind a bar with a big, cheesy grin on his face. There was another of Marian with crossed-eyes and Zach behind her making bunny ears. And there was one of Ava playing tennis with Zach at an indoor court.

Leith swiped to the texting function and chose Zach's name.

He tapped the little keyboard with his thumbs.

I'd like it if you could visit tomorrow.

Ten minutes later his phone beeped, and Zach's reply appeared on the screen.

I guess you're out of food? Missing that cheese already?

Smiling, Leith hit reply.

The food is welcome. You would be even more welcome.

Leith paused before hitting send, pondering if the comment seemed…odd. But he finally sent it. If Zach was his best friend then the idea that Leith wanted to see him wouldn't be unwanted. The response was almost immediate.

I'll be there. 10 am?

Excitement fluttered through Leith. He hadn't looked forward to anything but getting out of the hospital until now.

Whenever. I've got nowhere to go, unless you count art therapy. But my clay birds suck. I can skip it.

The reply from Zach came in a few heartbeats.

It's a date.

Leith smiled and leaned back, staring up at the ceiling. He remembered something, and texted Zach again.

Bring photos?

The reply took several minutes this time, but it finally came.

Sure. See you tomorrow.

Leith fluffed his pillow and turned out the light. In the dark he pretended the ceiling was the sky, and fell asleep counting imaginary stars.

TWO WEEKS EARLIER
VLOG ENTRY #2

INT. BLUE FLIGHT – BOOTH – NIGHT
Zach is pale. His eyes are red-rimmed, and he has a several-days-old beard.

ZACH

Hello, my loves.

He clears his throat.

I'm sorry for the delay in posting a vlog. I know—I promised to do a new one every week, and now... Now it has been two...two very long weeks. Sometimes each hour has felt like ten years, or an eon, or forever. Just endless. *Endless.*

His lips tremble, and he blinks rapidly.

Allow me to explain. As you remember, Leith was competing for the title of New York Amateur Boxing Champion. It was a difficult fight. His opponent—I don't even want to say his name. I won't say it.

He rubs his eyes.

Leith was well-matched. In fact, he was having the fight of his life. Though there were times I wasn't sure he was going to come out on top, he was still managing to land more punches than the other guy. Seeing him take a beating and keep going was exhilarating and excruciating all at once. Then... It happened at the end of the eleventh round. See, up until then Leith stood an excellent chance of winning.

His voice breaks.

But the asshole, he...well, Leith took an illegal blow to the back of his head.

Zach breaks off, and he covers his face with his hands, resting his elbows on the table. He looks at the screen again, his hands in his own hair.

It was so fast. The crowd was crazy. I was in the stands with our friends, and it took me so long to get through to the ring. Marvin, a fighter friend of Leith's, had to help me. By the time I got there...

He lifts his hands and lets them fall.

Leith was already unconscious. I don't remember a lot after that. The ambulance. The hospital. Don't worry, my loves, he's alive. I should've said that immediately, but...

He was in a coma, and I didn't know if he was going to live or die. The doctors wouldn't say anything—wouldn't give us any kind of reassurance. Just said, "Wait and see," and I had to sit there day and night looking at him, thinking that maybe it was all over. That I'd lost everything.

His face crumples.

40

I wasn't there when he woke up. Arthur was with him. I should have been there—maybe if I had... Maybe if he'd seen me first thing, but no. No, that isn't how it works. It wouldn't have mattered. It's unreal. It's like something you see on TV, but it's my *life*.

See, he's suffering from retrograde amnesia. The good news is, in terms of that kind of thing, he's not bad off. He's only lost approximately three years of memories. The last three years. Yeah, that's right. The three years that included me. He doesn't remember anything from that time—he doesn't remember me, or his prior girlfriends, or his father's death.

Zach lapses into silence, looking at the ceiling and then down at his hands, his lips twisting.

I hear that he's angry. Yes, that's right, I haven't seen him. It's been over a week now that he's been awake, and I'm being selfish. I should go see him. But I can't.

He hangs his head and rubs his eyes.

What's keeping me away from him? I bet most of you think you I'm an awful person that I'm not there with him to see him through this. I bet you're thinking nothing could keep you away from the one you love. You're right.

He lifts his head, and his eyes are wet.

41

I'm staying away because after he woke up they did some intake psych tests, and guess what? *He doesn't remember me.* Or even remember being bi. Can you believe it? He identified himself as straight. Without qualification, or hesitation, and didn't budge when gently questioned. Arthur told me. He was flabbergasted, and asked how I wanted him to deal with it. What I wanted him to say to Leith.

Tears run down his cheeks.

I can't...it's too much. No, no, you have to understand me. It's insane. In his mind, I've never touched him at all. I've never even existed. All that we had and were is just gone. Poof. Like it never happened at all.

So I told Arthur not to tell him yet, and the doctor said it was fine to wait since presenting him with information from his past won't affect his ability to retrieve his lost memories. They'll either return or not, and nothing we tell him about his past will change that. The doctor says we'll have to tell Leith the truth before we release him since everyone in his life will know about us, but... I said I wanted him to have a chance to know me again first, so it's not such a shock. Arthur pointed out that of course I have to go *see* Leith first for that to happen, but...

He shakes his head, sniffling.

Holy shit, guys. I'm scared. I've never been so

scared in my entire life, and I need him now. I need him more than I've ever needed him. And he's not here anymore. He's gone. Probably forever. *Forever!* What will I do? How can I go see him only to have him look at me and...and...

Zach sobs and he covers his face again. Eventually, he wipes at his eyes and clears his throat.

I'm sorry. I just wanted you to know what was happening. I don't know when I'll make another vlog post. I probably shouldn't unload all of this on strangers, but somehow it's easier than talking to my friends right now. But don't worry about me.

He smiles with false bravado.

I'll be fine. No matter what. And he'll be fine too. I'll see him soon—tomorrow maybe. I'll be brave, and I'll face the truth. I will, and then...we'll see.

His smile falters.

I just...I can't...

I love him.

Chapter Three

The girl in the photo was beautiful, with dark hair and hazel eyes, but she looked sad, even though she was smiling. "Were we happy?" Leith asked Zach.

After sitting stiffly in the chair and barely meeting Leith's eyes for the first ten minutes of his visit, Zach had kicked off his shoes, and sat opposite him, cross-legged on Leith's narrow hospital bed. The small box of photos rested between them.

He looked up at Leith, his eyes lit with something bright and hopeful, but then the light faded. "You and Naomi?"

"Yes," Leith replied, but he was distracted. He didn't know why, but he really liked the yellow polo shirt Zach was wearing. There was something compelling about it—not quite familiar, but like a stimulus that he recognized and somehow missed. He had a strange urge to reach out and feel the fabric.

"Did you used to wear that shirt a lot?" Leith asked, distracted from his original question by Zach's sober expression, and the yellow shirt again.

"No."

Zach sounded wounded, but Leith had no idea why. It was something that seemed to happen every few minutes, and Leith hated it. But he also liked having Zach around. It all left him feeling in need of a nap.

Zach said, "It's new. Janelle—my cousin—she bought it for me."

"Was it your birthday?"

"No. She was trying to butter me up for a favor."

"Did she get it?"

"No. I'm afraid she's in over her head again, and I'm not

going to bail her out every time she gets into trouble."

"Maybe you should give her a break. Sometimes people make mistakes," Leith said, thinking of his father's devastating gambling habit and his own two years in prison.

"Leith, you...well, perhaps hate is a strong word...but you deeply dislike Janelle."

"I do?"

"Yes, you truly do."

"Why?"

"Because she stole four thousand dollars from me and she's never paid it back. You wanted me to turn her in."

"Why didn't you?"

Zach's lips twisted a little and he shrugged. "She's my cousin. I keep thinking she'll turn it around and be a better person."

"Well, maybe she will."

Zach smiled a little. "God, I wish I could play back what you just said to you five months ago. You were hell bent on me calling the police then."

Leith considered. He must have had a good reason to want to turn the girl in, especially since he knew firsthand what it was like to get in trouble with the law. Maybe he shouldn't disagree with his old self too much. He rubbed his forehead, a small headache starting.

Frowning a little, Zach turned back to the stack of photos, pulling out another of Naomi. "You guys were dating when I first met you, but I don't know much about her."

Leith didn't look at the photo. His eyes were drawn back to the line of skin above the collar of Zach's shirt. "Even if I don't like your cousin, I like her taste in shirts. It suits you...and it looks soft. Can I touch it?"

Zach dropped the photo. Leith waited for an answer, aware

of the dust motes circling Zach's head, and the shimmer of the fragile skin of Zach's eyelids when he blinked.

"Sure."

Leith's stomach uncurled a little. He hadn't even realized he was holding his breath waiting for Zach's answer. Leith had no idea why he needed to feel the fabric beneath his fingers, but it felt important, key even, to finding some missing memory.

Leith reached out and stopped just short of skimming his fingers along the edge of Zach's collar, right next to that skin that looked like it would be soft and warm to touch. What was he doing? That was bizarre, and overly intimate.

He dropped his hand, deciding to take up the hem, but froze when he realized his fingers were mere inches from Zach's crotch. Finally he clapped his hand on Zach's shoulder in a manly gesture and smoothed his fingers over the fabric. It was soft, yes, but nothing happened. There was nothing in his mind that hadn't been there before.

The sensation of Zach's shoulder under his palm was strangely *good*. Zach held very still while Leith touched him, and the way Leith's eyes kept falling back to that sweet-looking spot on Zach's neck was distracting. And the fact that his cock was definitely a little heavier than it had been before he noticed these things was really fucking *weird*.

Leith cleared his throat and dropped his hand. "I don't know what that was about," he said, shaking his head. "Sometimes I just do stupid things now. Sorry. I hope that wasn't strange for you."

"Of course not. You can touch me whenever you want."

The sudden urge to kiss Zach's neck was insane. Leith took a shaky breath. "Did we used to, um, touch a lot?"

His fingers twisting together, Zach stared at his hands. "We were very close friends. Very comfortable with each other," He cleared his throat. "Do you want to see more photos, or should I pack these up?"

Leith picked up the second photo of the girl called Naomi. "She was my girlfriend?" She was certainly a sexy woman. It was odd that he wasn't more intrigued by the thought that he'd probably slept with her.

"Mm-hmm," Zach murmured, looking at the photo too. "Here, there's a better one of you two in here somewhere; one where you're both laughing."

Leith looked at the photo of him and Naomi. He zeroed in on his own face. He was indeed laughing, and his arm was slung around Naomi's slender shoulders. It could have been two strangers in the picture. There was nothing there inside him. "Was she nice?"

"Yeah. Like I said, I never knew her well, but Naomi was cool. Very smart. Funny. I liked her."

"Why did we break up?"

Zach hitched a shoulder and riffled through the box. "You weren't right for each other, I guess."

Leith picked up a photo of himself goofing around with Ava. Her chest was flushed, and he had his arm around her neck, his fingers grazing her cleavage. He felt a bit of a stirring when he considered that. Yes, that was more like it. "It looks like I'm good friends with Ava. Did we ever…?"

"You and Ava?" Zach's eyebrows shot up. "No. Definitely not."

"Why? Does she have a boyfriend?"

Zach took the photo from his hands and put it aside. "She's not your type."

Leith laughed a little. "Why? She's cute, she's nice, and she's available, right? How is that not my type?"

Rubbing his eyes with his fingertips, Zach let out a slow breath. "Because she's your friend. That's all."

"Are you sure?" He picked up the photo again. "I'm practically feeling her up here."

Zach's eyes flashed as he hopped off the bed. "There are names on the back of the photos, so you should be able to figure out who's in them without my help."

"But I won't know who they were to me..." Leith said, trailing off as Zach turned his back.

"I'm sorry, but I totally forgot about this thing I have to do. I really should go."

Leith watched in confusion as Zach bustled around putting on his shoes and grabbing his coat. There was something else that Leith was missing. He reviewed the last bit of their conversation. He'd said *something* wrong again, and it was about Ava, but not about Ava. It was about Ava being his type.

"Wait!" Leith climbed out of the bed and blocked the door. "Is Ava *your* type? Is that why I didn't date her?"

Zach shook his head, obviously bewildered. "No, Leith. Where is this coming from? Ava and I are friends, and you and Ava are friends, and nothing would have changed that. Marian and Ava, though? Are not friends. They're lovers."

"Really?" Leith pondered it. "We live with lesbians?"

Zach looked flustered again. With his hands waving around, he said, "Exactly. You and Ava are like brother and sister, and that's all there is to it." He was almost shouting.

"How was I supposed to know that?" His jaw clenching, Leith snapped, "Why didn't you just tell me? I don't fucking remember! Remember?"

Zach opened his mouth, eyes blazing, and then pressed his lips together, his shoulders slumping. He swallowed hard. "I'm sorry."

Leith sighed. "No, I'm sorry. I don't mean to be an asshole. I just...I feel like something's missing. I don't know how to explain it. But I *know* the most important part of understanding myself is right there out of reach, and I keep thinking that any second now it's all going to fall into place. But it doesn't."

Zach's face softened, and he stepped forward, putting his hand against Leith's cheek. It was big and warm, and Leith closed his eyes and leaned into it.

"Hey, hey," Zach murmured. "It's all right, Leith. I'm sorry—I should have just answered your questions instead of making you guess. Listen, even if you never get your memories of the last few years back, I have no doubt that the man you are inside is more than enough to build a beautiful life—with whomever you want, and however you want."

Leith wanted to press his forehead to Zach's and breathe in the smell of his cologne again. Instead he forced himself to step back and release Zach's arm. "Thank you. I just feel...really alone right now."

Zach draped his jacket on the chair, kicked off his shoes, and climbed back up onto the bed, patting the spot across from him.

"I thought you had somewhere to be?" Leith asked, scooting onto the bed too. It was good to sit again.

"It can wait. Everything else can wait."

Zach opened the box of photos again, and his hand looked incredibly strong and steady to Leith when he pulled out the next photo.

"This is you and me the day after I got back from a trip to Kentucky to see my mother," Zach said.

Leith took the photo. He and Zach stood together in an unfamiliar kitchen, both in T-shirts and sweatpants. Zach looked so much younger; so much happier; like there were no worries at all in his life. As for himself, he looked incredibly relaxed.

His stomach flip-flopped as he stared at the picture. There

was something about the way he was looking at Zach. The itching in his mind intensified, and he breathed shallowly. He thought about his body's reaction to being close to Zach. How he wanted to breathe Zach in, and touch his skin, and feel—

Leith's pulse raced, and his mouth went dry.

Zach glanced up from where he sorted through the photos. His brow creased. "Are you feeling okay? Maybe you should lie down." He reached for Leith's knee.

"No," Leith croaked. He grabbed a glass of water from the table beside him and gulped. He managed a smile even though it felt as if Zach's palm was burning him through the flannel of his pajama pants. "I'm fine."

He wondered if Zach knew that Leith had been in love with him.

INT. LEITH AND ZACH'S BEDROOM – NIGHT
Zach sits at a desk chair. There's a bed with crumpled sheets behind him. His eyes are puffy, and his hair is tousled.

ZACH

It's four in the morning. I can't sleep and I thought of you my loves, and all your concerned comments and emails. I'm sorry I haven't replied. I've barely been able to talk to anyone. My sister Maddie's worried about me. She calls every day. I know I should talk to her, but it's too much. As you might imagine, I'm not doing too well right now.

His eyes focus somewhere beyond the camera, and he shakes his head slowly.

I saw him. Leith. He...he's...fuck, he truly and completely doesn't remember me.

His voice cracks.

I don't know what to say about that. I keep thinking that any day now, any second, I'll wake up and this will be a terrible nightmare. And when I've seen him, I feel like I'm going to die if he doesn't look at me and know who I am. I feel so...

He shakes his head blankly.

Lost, and scared. And it's ridiculous, but I'm so angry because I...I'd know him anywhere. He looks at me like I'm a stranger.

I first went two days ago. Afterward I crawled into bed, and I couldn't get out until today. Because he asked to see me again, and how can I say no?

He sniffs loudly and shakes his head again.

He texted me, and I thought maybe, just maybe, something had come back to him. He wanted me to bring pictures of people he knows, and I did. Of course he wanted to know about his old girlfriend Naomi. It was torture. It was so hard to answer his questions, and he got mad at me. And I don't blame him for that. But I really wanted to yell back. I wanted to scream.

His voice trembles and breaks.

I feel betrayed. Can you believe that? He's injured—he could have *died*—and he lost his memory, and *I* feel betrayed? But that's how I feel. Like if he loved me enough there would have been nothing—nothing in the whole damn world that could erase me from his mind.

But seeing him...the look in his eyes? I'm gone. *We're* gone. We're nothing. Everything we had is dead. I love him so much, and it's all *gone*.

Zach's lips curl into a snarl before he bursts into tears.

I know it isn't his fault, but I'm still angry. I feel

so...broken. Like, fuck him. He forgot me? *Fuck him.*

He throws up his hands and closes his eyes.

I just wanted to forget. I wanted to forget and feel whole again. So I did what I used to do when I was a stupid kid. I wanted to lose myself, and I thought everything could be made easier with a stupid, meaningless fuck.

Zach indicates the bed over his shoulder as tears fall.

It worked. I forgot—for about ten minutes. And then it all came crashing down on me, and I feel like I can't breathe. It was pointless, beyond meaningless, and now...

His voice breaking, he whispers.

Now the sheets smell like another man, and I...I don't want to go on without him. Without Leith. He's everything to me. *Everything.* And he doesn't even know who I am! Would it hurt more if he was dead? Could it? I don't know. I don't know anymore.

Zach bows his head and his shoulders shake. There's a knock at the door, and Zach wipes at his face.

MARIAN (*off screen*)
Zach? Zach, can I come in?

ZACH

Sure.

He whispers to the camera.

Apologies, my loves, for the emotional breakdown. Goodnight.

Chapter Four

"So, I was going to college at CUNY," Leith repeated slowly around his bite of sandwich. Ham and swiss with all the fixings. He wasn't sure where Arthur had bought it because it'd been wrapped in standard shiny foil without a logo, but he felt sure that if Zach had come to visit him, the sandwich he'd have brought would've tasted better.

Not that Zach's come to visit me lately.

It had been a few days—four, actually—and Leith felt hurt one minute and relieved the next. He needed to get his head on straight before he saw Zach again. He huffed out a laugh. *Get my head on straight. So to speak.*

"What?" Arthur asked. "Why is that funny? You'd always planned to go to college before…"

"Before I landed in prison fresh out of high school because I'm an idiot? Anyway, I was going to CUNY."

Arthur nodded, picking the pickles off his hoagie. He shifted in the chair beside Leith's bed, crossing his legs. "Queens College for physical education. I never quite understood if you wanted to be a boxing instructor or teach gym to kids. I admit I never really listened when you talked about it."

Leith snorted.

"So which was it?" Arthur asked.

"I don't remember, asshole."

Arthur grinned, reaching over and taking a big bite out of Leith's sandwich and moaning like it was delicious. Leith wrinkled his nose. He was certain he'd had better—he just didn't know where.

"You should ask Zach if you really want to know," Arthur

said. "He listened to you talk about your hopes and dreams all the time. I don't know why, because they were always so pedestrian. But he seemed to enjoy it."

Leith flipped Arthur off until he'd chewed and swallowed again. "Oh, and your dreams are epic?"

"Well. You know me."

"Yes, what admirable dreams you have. Aspiring to spend even more time between even more women's thighs?" Leith wiped at one eye. "I'm so proud."

"Hey now. I'll have you know that my numerous sexual encounters with humans of the female kind are because I'm possessed of a deeply romantic, loving nature, thank you very much." He paused and couldn't hold back a grin. "And because God, I love sex."

Laughing, Leith took another bite of sandwich, and his mind went to that soft looking skin on Zach's neck, the brightness of his eyes, and the pink of his mouth. He took a big gulp of water. As he swallowed, an image of Zach's ass in those zipper-pocket jeans came to mind, and he had to take another sip to cool the heat that flared inside him.

How long had the Leith from before known he might be gay or bi or whatever these weird feelings meant? And what about Zach? He'd seemed a little feminine at times, but that didn't mean he was gay. It all made Leith want to scoot down in his bed and pull the covers over his head.

"But seriously," Arthur said. "CUNY's been amazing about all of this. They agreed to hold your place so you can rejoin the program again when you're well." He smirked. "Of course you'll have to start from scratch since you went and forgot everything you learned."

He rolled his eyes. "Who needs brains when you've got brawn and beauty?"

The truth was Leith was plenty smart—or he had been. He

still had no idea what the injury might have done to his IQ. Of course he knew that just because he could write a decent essay or appreciate poetry didn't mean he made smart life choices. Knowing the proper declension of Latin verbs, as he had in high school, hadn't led him to a life lacking in impulsive, bone-headed moves.

In fact, as far as Leith was concerned the ways in which he was smart had always been completely useless. Sure, he'd achieved top scores in school, but he'd still fucked up his life. Boxing was the only thing he'd ever been smart at in a way benefitted him, at last for a while. But as evidenced by his current predicament, he'd apparently still managed to mess up *everything* in the boxing ring. Or someone else had messed it up for him. The result was the same.

Arthur had always had his share of adventures, but they'd generally been of the romantic kind. He'd gotten into a lot less trouble than Leith over the years, so maybe those extra few IQ points he had over Leith *did* count for something.

Not meeting Arthur's eyes, Leith asked, "So, when I left prison, what happened?"

Arthur looked up, concerned little furrows appearing between his brows. "We've discussed this before."

"I know. I remember. I just want to hear it again."

Arthur shrugged, eating one of the pickles he'd picked off earlier. "Well, like I've said, you came to live with me but in the end you couldn't stand my mess, so you moved in with Marian. You'd met her at CUNY."

"How? In class?"

"I don't know. You'll have to ask her. Then Ava moved in a couple of months later when she and Marian got hot and heavy." Arthur smirked. "For a while, right after the break up with Naomi, I thought you were totally hitting that. *Both* of that, if you get my meaning."

57

Leith waggled his eyebrows, even though his heart wasn't in it.

"I was pretty impressed with your new and sudden prowess with the ladies. Of course, I should have known better."

"I'm plenty man for two women."

It was Arthur's turn to roll his eyes. "Like I said, I'd have known better if I'd really given it more thought. But you were being so secretive at the time. I had to come up with *some* explanation, and I suppose that was the most titillating one."

Arthur always did like to talk like a professor. With all the potential for sexual escapades with students, Leith sometimes wondered if his brother hadn't dodged a bullet by never going down that path. Despite multiple scholarship offers, Arthur had never gone to school at all, striking out on his own in New York City with the small inheritance he had from their mother's death. Leith's was long gone, gambled away by their father, for which Leith had no one to blame but himself.

Leith remembered with pride how Arthur had gotten that first small bar, Joseph's Teeth, off the ground before Leith even graduated high school. It was named for the bloody end result of the only punch Arthur had ever landed on Joseph Tiernan, a bully from Arthur's gangly, scarecrow teen years.

The bar had been more successful than Arthur had ever imagined. He'd paid off old debts, hired full-time staff, and offered to help Leith with school. But he'd refused to loan even a dime to help their father. Leith frowned, fighting off the residual anger he felt about that, reminding himself that it was all bygones now. After all, his father was long dead, even if it felt like only weeks to him.

His mind back on the conversation, Leith thought to ask, "What was I being secretive about?"

Arthur shrugged. "Whatever it was, you definitely weren't sharing your little man with Marian and Ava."

"What makes you so sure? I'm pretty good looking. I might've been able to work it."

Arthur scoffed. "I know *you* think you're awfully pretty, and I guess you are, but you can't turn rug-munchers straight. Besides, Marian would never have asked you to move in if she thought you'd want to sleep with her. She's level-headed, that girl. And, *even if* they'd been interested, you were never much of a ladies' man. Not like that. Even though you could have been." Arthur suddenly became very absorbed in trying to scrape excess mustard off his sandwich.

"I had girlfriends."

Arthur shrugged.

He studied Arthur carefully, noting how his brother avoided looking him in the eyes now. "Was I in love with Naomi? Or was it more casual than that?"

Arthur's face made it plain that he'd been skeptical. "I heard you tell Naomi you loved her a few times."

"But did I *really* love Naomi?"

"I assume you must have. Why else would you have told her you did?"

"There are different kinds of love, though. I love you, for example."

"True."

Leith cleared his throat, prompting Arthur.

"Fine, fine. You're okay, I guess. For a little brother who does dumb shit like get thrown in prison, and then scares the shit out of me by getting his brains scrambled in a boxing match."

"Um, thanks." It wasn't really what he'd wanted Arthur to say. He'd wanted him to go back to speculating about Leith's feelings for Naomi and what kind of love he might have had for her.

"You're welcome." Arthur paused, rolled his eyes, and then sighed. "You know I love you."

"Yeah."

"You're my family, and I love you just the way you are, brain scrambled former-felon and all."

"I know. You don't suck either."

Arthur ate in silence as Leith turned over another question, trying to decide if he should ask. His stomach knotted, and he forced a breath. "What about Zach?" he blurted. The segue was terrible but Leith had never been subtle.

Arthur flicked his gaze up warily. "What about him?"

"Did I love him?" His heart pounded.

Arthur blinked. "I'm sorry?"

Leith chickened out. "Friends love each other, right? A different kind of love."

Arthur swallowed, his eyes darting to the side. "Yes. Of course." He smiled and met Leith's gaze. "You were very close. Why? I thought you couldn't remember Zach?"

"I can't. I don't. I just...he seems like a really great guy." He'd said the same thing to Marian and Ava. He didn't know how else to describe the source of the confusing tangle of feelings inside. "What's he like?"

"He's a good partner in Blue Flight. Dependable. Smart. If you want to know more about Zach, you should ask Zach," Arthur said, reasonably. "He wouldn't mind."

Leith bit into his sandwich and chewed, trying to think of how he could ask the right question. Did Arthur know? Had Leith shared his feelings with his older brother? Arthur had never been homophobic, but it was different when it was your family, wasn't it?

"Did you know that if it hadn't been for that asshole who put you in this place, you'd have been the New York amateur boxing champion?"

"You told me. That's...insane. I wish I could remember."

"It *was* kind of crazy. But you worked for it. No one deserved it more than you."

Leith knew that Arthur had changed the subject on purpose, and he let him. He wasn't sure he was ready to share his discovery that he'd been in love with Zach before the accident. As much as he wanted to know if Zach had been aware of his feelings—or even more terrifying, if the vast amount of affection he sensed had been returned at all, another part of him felt nauseous and shaky.

Especially when he didn't understand why his former self had felt these things for Zach. He might not remember whether or not he'd loved Naomi, but he remembered his first love in high school, and she had been decidedly female. The idea that he might be gay or bi was so unexpected that he couldn't bring himself to say the words out loud. Not yet.

So if Arthur wanted to talk about boxing, Leith would let him.

When Arthur finally left, Leith lay back in his bed and tried to decide if he'd made the right choice to not ask more about Zach. *Maybe I should just ask Zach myself.*

After several minutes of agonizing, he grabbed the phone and tapped out a text to Zach.

Can I see you tomorrow?

Leith's foot jiggled as he waited, staring at the screen and willing a response.

I'm not sure. The schedule at the bar fell apart unexpectedly.

Leith stared at the words and pondered the cold disappointment that seeped into him. He wanted to see Zach so badly that even waiting until tomorrow had seemed too long. Now he might not even get that. He thumbed a request into his phone and hesitated, wondering if it sounded as weird as he thought it probably did. Finally, he pressed send.

Send me a picture of you right now?

It took more than a minute for Zach to respond.

Why?

It was a good question. Leith stared at the screen for a long moment before replying.

I miss you.

His pulse pounded, and his hands shook. When his phone vibrated and the picture popped up, Leith examined it closely. He quickly replied.

You look tired. Are you okay?

He waited for a response, and as the seconds ticked by he second guessed himself. Had he offended Zach by saying he looked tired? He didn't mean to insult him. He was just concerned by the dark circles under Zach's eyes. Maybe—

His phone vibrated.

Is this better?

Leith bit down on his lip grinning as the second picture popped up. Zach was so damn handsome. He'd taken the picture himself with his phone, and his eyes looked greenish-blue above the light brown sweater he was wearing and his expression was playful—narrowed eyes that showed off his long, black lashes, and a twisted smirk to his lips, like he was making fun of Leith for the photo request.

He wanted to ask for another one, but he didn't think he could. He ran his finger over Zach's close-shaven cheek in the picture and he wondered what it would feel like against his lips. Another message appeared.

Where's mine?

Leith blinked at the words.

You want a picture of me?

The three little dots appeared, and he held his breath.

Fair's fair.

A thrill shot down Leith's spine. Was this flirting? This wasn't like conversations he usually had with other guys. Shouldn't Zach be asking him about the Yankees vs. the Red Sox or something? Shouldn't they call each other "dude" or "bro" and text each other insults?

He fiddled with the phone until he figured out how to take a picture of himself. He tried out several different expressions, not sure exactly what would be best. First a smile, but that seemed too fake. Second a smirk like Zach, but that seemed like he might be making fun. Finally he settled for one with his eyes crossed and his tongue out. He included a comment with the picture: *I'm bored.*

Clearly. You're terrible at making your own fun.

Another picture came through, and this time it was Zach with a napkin on his head and two straws twisted together and held over his lip like a mustache. Leith laughed, happiness crashing over him in a tingly wave as he replied.

You win. I can't beat that.

Leith held the phone, waiting. When a reply didn't materialize within a few minutes he studied the photos, wondering what Zach did for fun, and what sorts of things Zach liked. Did Zach like Mexican food? Or Thai? Or Italian? Or how about bratwurst? Leith had surely known, and now he had no idea.

Gazing at Zach's goofy picture, he desperately wanted to know the answers again. Did he listen to classical music or heavy metal? No, looking at Zach's picture, Leith felt sure he liked pop music, and he guessed the more diva the performer the better. He closed his eyes and allowed himself to imagine Zach dancing and singing to some old school Madonna, maybe "Like a Prayer."

The lyrics of the song came unbidden to mind, and the image of Zach on his knees made him feel hot and cold all at once. He jumped as his phone came to life.

Sorry. Busy here. More later.

Leith was disappointed all over again, but he settled back against his pillow and let himself drift. He moved away from the overwhelming image of Zach on his knees—his long fingers on the button of Leith's jeans, and his hot green eyes with the hint of blue staring up—to the more mundane, easier-to-breathe-through image of Zach simply walking into his room. This...this Leith could deal with. He could imagine it perfectly.

Zach would take off his coat and drape it over the chair like always. But what would he say? First he'd *smile*. Leith knew that for sure. He decided it would be the genuine smile, the one Leith liked best, and not the tentative, anxious one that Zach wore too often.

Maybe Zach would come over to the bed and bend close to him. Perhaps he'd put his hand in Leith's hair, and whisper, "I'm so glad to see you."

Leith shifted, his body humming with longing and strange satisfaction. Yes, this was right. These thoughts felt good. Natural. He imagined Zach bending even lower, brushing his lips against Leith's forehead—no! His mouth. He would kiss Leith on the mouth, and his lips would be—

Leith groaned. *How* would they be? Discovering that he had *feelings* for Zach, inexplicable and urgent feelings, was incredibly exciting. But it was confusing too. He'd felt strong, exciting things for men sometimes when he was younger--Sweets Swinson being the most compelling of them all--but he'd always dismissed it as hero-worship. The idea that he might be gay should bother him. He'd never been one to deal with change well, and this was a huge change. But for some inexplicable reason he didn't have any desire to deny it. Why? Maybe he had accepted it before the accident?

He wondered who he could ask.

Had he kept these feelings secret? He must have. Who would he have told? He supposed Zach would have been the best candidate, but since he'd been in love with him surely he wouldn't have risked their friendship with that kind of admission?

He was desperate to hear from Zach again already. He thumbed in a reply, probably too intense and too soon, and sent it before he could stop himself.

I really miss you.

There was no reply, and he hadn't really been expecting one. After all, Zach had a bar to run and it was Friday night. But he still held the phone against his chest until he fell asleep. When he woke the next morning with the phone pressed into his side, he smiled blearily at the message time stamped well after midnight but waiting patiently for him.

I really miss you too.

The rain rushed by Dr. Thakur's office windows. It was dark in the room without the sun shining, and the gloom lent a solemn atmosphere to the usually cheerful room. Dr. Thakur sat at his desk, a big wooden thing that made him seem very small behind it. There were photos of his wife and children scattered around, and loads of books with titles that made Leith's head swim.

"You've been much calmer this week, but also more distant. The OTs all report that you've been subdued. Can you tell me about what's going on with you?"

Leith leaned back in the leather chair, trying to decide what he wanted to tell Dr. Thakur. His whole perspective had altered, and he didn't know where to start.

"I'm just thinking of the future I guess," Leith said. "Arthur told me that CUNY was holding my place, and I don't know if I want to go back. And then there's boxing. I don't know how to feel about it. I used to love it, but I don't know if I should fight again. I don't know if I want to. This injury was a close call."

Dr. Thakur looked at his file and closed it. "Speaking of such things, you've been cleared for more rigorous exercise. Would you like to start using the gym here tomorrow? I think it would be a good source of stress relief for you."

"Sure. That sounds good."

Dr. Thakur sat behind his desk looking as calm and radiant as always. Leith idly wondered if he ate stars for breakfast to glow like that, and then his thoughts turned, as they had all week, back to Zach. He also glowed like he was made of starlight, so pale and bright.

"Zach brought pictures for me to look at the other day."

"Did you find them of interest?"

"Yes." Leith looked down at his hands folded in his lap. "His full name is Zachariah. That's a nice name, don't you think?"

"It is indeed. Did you know it means 'Jehovah remembers'?" Dr. Thakur smiled, his white teeth flashing. "Are you aware, Leith, of the various threads of meaning in your name? Given the situation, you mind find them interesting."

"My mother chose my name. Her people were Scottish," Leith said. "My father's side was German."

"I see. Perhaps the connection exists only in my mind then."

Leith waited, but Dr. Thakur said nothing else. "So you're not going to share? You're just going to drop something like that into our session and expect me to ignore it?"

"Not ignore it. Ponder it, maybe. But if you're curious, have you ever heard of the River Lethe? No? According to Greek myth, it was one of the five rivers in the Greek underworld. The dead were forced to drink from the waters of Lethe in order to erase their memory of their life on earth."

"I haven't heard of it."

"According to the Greek beliefs, some might say that during the time you were in a coma you traveled to the underworld, consumed the water of Lethe, and then returned instead of going on across the River Styx. Some might say that's how you came to lose your memories."

He scoffed. "Who would say that?"

"Long ago Greeks, perhaps."

"Well, some might say that you're stranger than any of your patients."

Dr. Thakur grinned. "Indeed. I think we both agree *some* would be right on that account. But consider it a moment, Leith. The waters of Lethe. Is there a lesson in the concept of the river of forgetting you can embrace?"

"Don't drink the Kool-Aid?"

"Nicely played," Dr. Thakur said. "But don't sell yourself short here, Leith. Give it some thought."

Leith crossed his arms over his chest and shrugged.

"In the meantime, you were telling me about Zachariah—"

"Jehovah remembers."

"—and how you liked his name."

Leith shrugged. He'd lost the thread of his original comment. His mind drifted back to Zach and the way his hands moved when he talked, and the exciting sound of his laugh. He wished he could remember what had attracted him to Zach the first time. Had it been there from the beginning? Or had it been a gradual fall? How had he taken it, he wondered? Because he wasn't sure he would have taken it well. He'd always focused his attention on women. He'd never allowed himself to seriously consider a man before.

Leith sighed.

"Sounds heavy," Dr. Thakur said.

"I just wish I could remember."

"I know. It would make things simpler, I'm sure."

If he was Lethe, a river of forgetting, and Zach was about remembering, what did that mean? Who exactly was Jehovah—was that another name for God?—and what was it he remembered? Everything? Or nothing?

Dr. Thakur cleared his throat. "That's all for today, Leith. I'm sorry to cut our session short, but my son has a football tournament this afternoon, and I promised I'd attend." He frowned at the window. "They play rain or shine, I'm afraid."

Leith stood up and ran his hands over the jeans Arthur had brought in the day before. Leith felt like it was progress to start dressing in real clothes again. Arthur had also brought shirts, including a blue polo that was very similar to the yellow one Zach had worn. "It's from Zach," Arthur had told him. "He thought you'd like it."

Leith had rubbed the fabric against his cheek. "Yeah. It's soft." He must have sounded strange because Arthur had made a face at him. Now, Leith crossed over to Dr. Thakur's door, and he smoothed his hand over the front of his shirt, remembering the way Zach's shoulder had felt against his palm.

"Leith? One last thing. What is the significance of the birds you keep making in art therapy? Do you know?"

Leith fiddled with the hem of his shirt. "I think I just like birds."

Dr. Thakur's eyebrows lifted, and it was clear he didn't believe him, but Leith walked out anyway. He made his way to the door to the rose garden. He stood in the open threshold and listened to the drone of the rain.

After several minutes of feeling the spray of it against his face as it pelted the sidewalk, Leith pulled his cell phone from his pocket and texted Zach.

My doctor wants to know why I keep making birds out of clay in art therapy.

Zach's reply made him smile, and he put the phone away. He stepped into the rain, feeling it seep into his hair, run down his face, and soak his clothes. He felt clean and cheerful. He felt good. He repeated Zach's message in his head, hearing the text in Zach's voice.

Has it never crossed his mind that you might simply like birds?

THE SAME DAY
VLOG ENTRY #4

INT. APARTMENT – COUCH – DAY
Zach sits on a sofa in an apartment alone. Behind him is a table strewn with dishes.

ZACH
Hello, my loves! It's your old friend Zach here. Thank you, my dear friends, for the unbelievably kind and loving comments and emails. It's in part because of you that I feel so much more optimistic today. Thank you especially to everyone who even offered me places to stay so I could get away from it all. In other circumstances, that would have been just the break that I needed.

I even bought a plane ticket to visit a friend in Italy! I had the ticket printed out and my bag packed, I'd thrown Blue Flight into Arthur's hands—even though he's got more than enough on his plate these days too. And then...

He shrugs and sighs, looking up at the ceiling and then back at the camera with a sparkle in his eyes.

Well, then Leith texted me. What can I say? I sat forever right here on this very sofa, just staring at the words he'd sent, and I knew I couldn't go.

He said he missed me.

He takes a deep breath and blows it out slowly.

You can imagine how it felt to hear that. I owe it

to Leith to stay and see him through his mess in whatever capacity I can. And as much as I'd love to jet off to Italy and drown my sorrows in Chianti, it wouldn't be fair to Arthur—or the staff at the bar. They've all been so great about pitching in since the accident. I guess the days have passed when I can pretend to be carefree and without responsibilities.

He smiles sadly.

Carefree. It's hard to imagine I ever felt that way. So...I guess you're wondering, aren't you? How things are with Leith?

He shrugs, pressing his lips together, and looking down.

Things are much the same, but entirely different. He doesn't remember me. That hasn't changed. I'm told that it never will. But *I* remember *him*, and I love him. I made a big mistake earlier this week, thinking that being with another man could help somehow. It was so tempting to keep running, but then Leith texted. If *he* misses *me*, then maybe...

He shakes his head.

No. I can't let myself go down that road. But just because he doesn't remember all the promises we made to each other doesn't mean I shouldn't keep them. We might not have been married, but we'd promised to take care of each other no matter what, and I'm holding myself to that. I'll

71

never stop doing things for Leith. No matter what. No matter how this turns out.

Zach sighs, picks up a throw pillow from the couch, and then tosses it aside. He grabs it back and leaves it in his lap, his fingers twisting at the seam.

He thinks I'm his best friend. That was what the doctor and I agreed on when they said I could see him finally. It's true enough but it leaves out a lot, obviously.

And it's hard because every time I see him, I want to kiss him and touch him the way I used to, but I can't. I don't even mean sex. It's everything else that I miss so much more. Things like...how soft his hair felt when I mussed it, and the way he smelled, and the rumble of his voice in his chest when I lay with my head on it at night...

Biting his lip, he shakes his head.

I can't allow myself to think of those things right now. It doesn't do any good, and it hurts.

He slaps his palms against the pillow.

So I'm moving forward. How will I move forward, you may ask? Well, I'm going to see Leith every day starting tomorrow. I know, it's not exactly what most people consider to be moving on, but it's what I have to do. He needs me, and I'm not going to let myself be a coward anymore.

He takes a deep breath and smiles shakily.

So that's where I'm at, my lovelies. A better place than the last time you heard from me. It's progress, and I'll take it. I'm nervous about going back to see Leith, but I'm excited too. I'd go now if visiting hours weren't ending soon, but tomorrow will have to do. I'll let you know how it goes. Until then, farewell.

He blows a kiss to the camera.

Chapter Five

Arthur, skinny and tired-looking as ever, trimmed Leith's hair with old-fashioned clippers while he talked about the two hundred dollars he'd lost on the horses.

"That looks better," he said, cleaning up the mess and wiping a warm, wet towel over Leith's neck and shoulders. "Hop in the shower so you don't itch."

Leith washed himself while Arthur stood in the doorway, describing the neck-and-neck final moments that had put his horse in second place. "Hindsight being what it is, I should have gone for the exacta box. I'd have walked away with a little money, at least."

"You're playing with fire," Leith said, drying off and pulling on fresh clothes. "After our father's problems you shouldn't be betting on horses at all, Arthur."

His brother waved his hand. "Hold *your* horses, baby brother. It was just a day of fun with a pretty lady."

"Oh? You have a pretty lady?"

"Don't I always?" Arthur smirked, brushing his hair out of his face.

Leith chuckled to himself. *If anyone needs a trim…*

A knock at the door announced Zach, who stood laden down with bags and a big basket. His dark hair was in impeccable order, and he wore an aqua, tight-fitting T-shirt that made his pale skin appear luminescent. He smiled tentatively.

"You came back!" Leith blurted. He cleared his throat, willing his heart to stop racing. "Hey. Good to see you."

"Your food dealer has arrived, baby brother," Arthur said, watching as Zach put his bundles on the comfy chair in the corner. "Speaking of addictions, I'm sure he's feeding yours."

"Cheese?" Leith asked.

"Of course," Zach answered, his dark pink lips widening to reveal his bright teeth.

Leith watched closely as Arthur slung an arm around Zach's shoulders and shook him the same way he did Leith. Leith noted with satisfied amusement that spread warm and right through his body that Arthur didn't have to stand on his tip-toes to give the brotherly shake since he and Zach were roughly the same height.

Zach let Arthur man-handle him without any fuss, and then started unpacking the picnic basket, revealing fresh fruit, a new container of yogurt, and bright vegetables that made Leith's mouth water.

Arthur said, "Since Zach's here for dinner, that means Blue Flight has been left in the hands of our employees, so I'd better get over there and supervise."

"Oh yes, that's the only reason you'd want to rush over," Zach said, rolling his eyes.

"You know as well as I do that one of us should always be there," Arthur said with a haughty air.

"Uh-huh." Zach smirked. "Then you'd better get moving."

Leith watched the exchange with a small smile. Before he could ask who his brother wanted to rush over to see, Arthur cuffed Leith on the head lightly—*very* lightly.

"I'll be on my way. Mind your ps and qs, mister. Use your manners, don't flirt with too many nurses, and be a good boy for Zach while I'm away."

Leith felt his cheeks heat a little at that ridiculous show, but Zach didn't seem to find it odd. In fact he wasn't really paying attention as he pulled out a clean blanket and unfolded it, eyeing the floor on the other side of Leith's bed like he was going to spread it there.

"Bye," Zach called absently as Arthur slipped out the door and shut it behind him with a click.

Leith was glad he'd gone. He didn't think Zach knew the way Leith was reacting to his presence, but he definitely didn't want Arthur to pick up on it. Not until he'd figured out why or how this was happening to him.

"I brought a picnic," Zach said, smiling as he spread the blanket out on the floor space he'd been considering. "All kinds of good things from the market and some sandwiches from your favorite deli."

He wanted to hug Zach, but he didn't know if that was something they'd done as friends. *Hadn't Arthur said to hug him when Zach first visited?* Still, Leith hesitated. He hovered, awkward and yearning, behind Zach as he opened the picnic basket and pulled out what looked like a tinfoil-wrapped hoagie.

Leith reached for it eagerly, his stomach rumbling, but Zach held the sandwich back, gesturing at the blanket on the floor.

"Grab a pillow," Zach said. "You'll be more comfortable."

"What else did you bring?" Leith asked, throwing his two bed pillows on the blanket and sitting on one.

Zach folded his legs and sat across from him, transferring the basket and bags to the ground next to him. "Hmm, some comfortable changes of clothes, Oreos, and let's see, oh, a big container of mac and cheese from Mac Shack. Do you remember how much you love it?"

Leith chuckled and shook his head.

"Well, you do."

"I'm glad someone knows what I like," Leith said. "I'm glad *you* know what I like."

Zach's pale skin grew slightly pink, but he just shrugged. "You'll know what you like again soon enough."

He handed over the hoagie, and Leith unwrapped it carefully. His mouth rushed with saliva as the tangy scent of mustard and pickles hit his nose, and he took a big bite. He moaned, not caring that a blob of mustard dripped onto his sweatpants. "God, this is so much better than what Arthur brought yesterday."

"Arthur likes the gross deli on fifth." Snickering, Zach shuddered. "You like City Sub, but you have to walk a little farther for it." He reached into the basket to pull out another container. It was creamed corn—another of Leith's favorites from childhood. He whimpered as Zach popped a spoon into the container and shoved it his way.

"Here," Zach said. "You love this too."

Leith put aside his sandwich and tasted the delicious creamed corn. He'd known Zach would bring him better food than Arthur. He wondered what else Zach knew about him. Yet he knew nothing at all in return...only these intense feelings of attraction and affection, unmoored in any facts.

"What's your mother's name?" Leith asked, desperately fetching the first question that came to mind.

"Melody," Zach said. "Why?"

"You never talk about yourself. I don't really know anything about you, and you seem to know everything about me. That isn't fair, is it?"

"Okay. What do you want to know?" Zach asked, opening up his own sandwich and picking off the olives.

"You don't like olives?"

"I do, just not with this cheese."

"Hmm," Leith said, thinking for a moment. He wanted to ask why Zach made his heart ache and his blood sing. Instead, he went with, "How did you and Arthur become partners in Blue Flight?"

"Well, that's an easy one." Zach grinned, and then took a moment to eat a bite of his sandwich before answering. "When I first moved into the apartment, I was still working for my sister. She owns a restaurant in Harlem. It's called Lisbet. Anyway, Maddie has a tendency to get distracted when her personal life goes to hell." Zach snorted softly. "Some might call that a family trait, actually."

Leith wanted to ask about that but Zach barreled on ahead. "I managed the restaurant for her while she went through a very messy divorce followed by a poorly chosen rebound love affair."

"Huh."

"Yeah. So, when she finally showed back up ready to reclaim all the duties of owner, as well as all the profits, I mentioned my frustrations about the lack of true advancement opportunities at Lisbet to Arthur." Zach's eyes flashed to Leith's and held them for a moment, as though he was waiting for him to say or do something. But then he simply went on to say, "By that time, I knew Arthur through you."

"Arthur offered you a job?"

"Yes. Blue Flight was doing so well and Arthur had just taken up…well, let's just say he had bigger fish to fry than managing a bar in Park Slope."

"What kind of fish?"

Zach waved the question off. "You know Arthur. It's always something. He bought a hovel in Queens to fix up, which he turned around for quite the profit, and then he had a new girl, and then another new girl." Zach snorted and rolled his eyes. "And then he was looking into buying a parking lot for a while. That fell through. In the end we made an agreement: I'd work as manager of the bar for three months, and if I did a suitable job, he'd let me buy in as a true partner."

"And you met his expectations?"

Zach chuckled. "Absolutely. Though recently our

employees have really taken up the slack. Arthur's incredibly dedicated, but he's got his mind on other things."

"Like...?" Leith could only imagine the enterprises his older brother might be into now.

Zach cleared his throat. "You, for one. It's been stressful for him since your accident. Anyway, back to Blue Flight—he let me buy in. It was the start of what was the absolute happiest year of my life. If I could find a way to live in that year forever, I would."

Feeling like he was channeling the group counselor, Leith prompted, "Why is that?"

Zach shrugged, gazing down at the blanket for a long, strangely sad moment. "It was just a good year, Leith. I was happy. Everything was perfect. Of course I didn't know it then. Hindsight is always twenty-twenty, isn't it?"

"I wouldn't know. I'm lacking a few years' worth of hindsight." He tried to make it sound funny, but Zach didn't laugh.

"Yeah. You are. Anyway, it's hard to explain."

"Oh." Leith looked at him thoughtfully. He could tell Zach didn't want to talk about that happy year, and he didn't know why. "So, you're not happy anymore?"

The corners of Zach's mouth went tight, and he swallowed. "Of course I'm happy. I've still got my bar—and hey, look! You're alive! For a while we weren't even sure of that. What more could I ask for?"

Zach smiled, but it wasn't the easy, beautiful smile Leith craved to see. Leith pondered the question for a moment, but when Zach's eyes flitted away from his nervously, he moved on to a less fraught topic. "Are you from New York originally?"

"No." Zach's lips quirked. "I know it's not as strong as it used to be, but I've still got a Southern accent, don't I?"

Leith swallowed. He'd noticed. The soft, rounded syllables and the occasional twang did things to his stomach—and his dick—so much so that he couldn't bring himself to confirm the fact that he'd noticed Zach's accent for fear of blushing.

"I grew up in Louisville," Zach went on. "But my family—we aren't very close. It's really just me and Maddie. My mother and I don't get along...even though I tried. A year ago I went down to see her, but it was just the same old thing. I'm not who she wants me to be, and she isn't who I need her to be. So we don't talk."

"There was a picture of us—you and me—after you came back from that trip to see your mother, right?" It was like memorizing a script or a novel; so many little pieces he had to keep track of.

"Yes," Zach answered.

Leith really wanted to ask more about that, but Zach's face closed off again and he got the impression that pressing the issue would be hurtful. "You're still close with Maddie even though you left the restaurant?"

"Yeah. There are no hard feelings there. She's proud of me for going after my dreams. I see her often enough." He jumped up and grabbed the old portable DVD player he'd brought in. "Speaking of my family, Maddie lent this to me. Can you believe she still has one? I was going to bring in the iPad and choose something from Netflix, but she thought you might want to see a familiar movie. Something you might have liked from before the accident." Zach handed Leith a wallet of old DVDs. "You choose."

Leith flipped through them, noticing that most of them were many years old, and they were all favorites of his. "How did you know I liked these movies?"

"It's *your* wallet of DVDs, Leith. I just brought it in. There was nothing magical about it."

80

Leith wondered if Zach believed he'd successfully diverted Leith from asking questions, and if Zach thought Leith didn't know that was what he was doing. As he studied each DVD, he wondered if Zach's reticence to discuss himself was because of *Leith* or because of himself. "What's this one?" Leith asked, stopping at a disc he'd never seen before. A movie called *Beautiful Thing*.

"How about *Rocky?*" Zach said, taking the wallet out of Leith's hands. "I haven't seen that in a long time."

Leith thought Zach was lying.

Zach went on, almost babbling, "It'll be comforting to see something you already know, right? And the message is inspiring, which is obviously what we need right now."

Leith took the wallet back, and looked at the photo on the front of disc he'd been looking at. It was two teenage boys with their arms around each other. "You don't think I'll like this one? I thought these were my movies."

"They are," Zach said, helplessly.

"Let's watch it. I want to see something new actually."

Zach shook his head and stood up, dusting his hands together. "It's getting late. You're tired and—"

"It's not late, Zach, and I'm not tired. Don't you like this movie?"

"No, I do. I just..."

"Please stay."

"I just think you'd probably enjoy it more alone, and I have a lot of things to do for work tomorrow morning." Zach yawned and stretched. "I'm tired, and it's a long trip back to the apartment. I should get going so I can hit the hay early."

"You could stay here tonight." Leith was gripping the DVD wallet tightly, and his heart thumped. What was he doing? Why was he asking Zach to stay? Zach hesitated and Leith plunged ahead, "I'll tell my nurse to bring in a cot for you. She won't mind. Or you could sleep on the fold-out chair. Arthur says it's pretty comfortable."

Zach's voice was breathy. "I wish I could, but I really need to go. Visiting hours are..." He trailed off.

"Is your girlfriend waiting for you?"

Zach shook his head. He pulled on his jacket, not meeting Leith's eye. "No, nothing like that."

"Do you have someone special?"

Zach turned his back as he packed up his few things. "I don't know. It's complicated."

"Please stay and watch the movie with me. I know I'm being selfish. It'll make it harder for you in the morning, but I like having you here. I've been lonely. Zach, when you're here...for some reason I don't feel so lonely."

Zach turned, and Leith felt a flood of warmth open in his chest when he realized Zach was going to stay.

"Okay. A little while longer."

Leith smiled and stood, taking Zach into the hug he'd been longing for since Zach first walked in the room. "Thank you."

Zach made a soft noise, and Leith turned his face toward Zach's neck a little, searching for the scent that he could almost remember. Zach held very still in his arms, and Leith could feel Zach's heart pounding against his own chest. As Leith let go, he whispered to Zach, "I'm glad we're friends."

"Me too," Zach said, his voice small and tender.

"Zach?" Leith stopped himself short of asking. He really wanted to know, and it was aching inside of him like a bruise he couldn't stop pressing against, but he didn't think he could handle it if Zach rejected him now. It was more than a little scary having these reactions and feelings tied to someone he didn't even know. Zach stood with his arms crossed over his chest, and

Leith's stomach twisted to see him so wary.

"Yes?"

Leith couldn't ask him the real question. He couldn't ask if Zach had known what Leith used to feel for him, and he couldn't ask if it was okay for him to still feel the same way. "What's your favorite color?"

"Red."

"I like blue," Leith said.

"I know," Zach whispered.

For them to both watch the movie on the tiny screen, Zach squeezed onto Leith's bed with him. When they both leaned back on the doubled up pillows, their heads were very close, and their bodies touched from toe to hip to shoulder.

Leith knew without a doubt that there had never been another male friend in his life, not since his childhood anyway, who would have shared this kind of close physical proximity without any manly shoulder punching or "no homo" jokes. But Zach settled against him without apology. Leith almost moaned at how right, solid, and comforting the weight of him was.

He had to close his eyes a moment while Zach fiddled with the DVD player to deal with the strange, urgent tightness in his throat. Tears rose on a current of emotion, and he wanted to turn on his side, wrap his arms around Zach and bury his face in the crook of his neck, breathing him in.

Leith held still, though his heart thudded so hard he imagined he could see his chest vibrating with each beat through his thin T-shirt. He noticed Zach's fingers shaking as Zach slid the DVD into the machine and pressed a button.

Before he could stop himself, Leith grabbed hold of Zach's hand and pressed it to his chest, holding it against his heart. The long, handsome fingers felt right there, touching him. Zach stilled, and Leith let go, heat rushing hard up his neck and into his face. He couldn't look at Zach.

"I'm sorry," he said. "I do really weird things now. It's like my body just does what it wants sometimes. I don't know why."

"It's okay." Zach swallowed thickly. "Don't worry about it. The movie's starting."

Leith chanced a glance at Zach, and found his greenish eyes warm and tired, but not at all offended. He smiled, and Zach turned slightly on his side, curling his hands up under his chin. Leith had to tear his eyes away in order not to miss the opening of the film.

The beginning of the movie was a little confusing and chaotic to Leith, made all the more so by the thick British accents. He was embarrassed that he had a hard time deciphering them, and was tempted to turn on the closed captioning to make sure he wasn't missing any important plot points. It seemed strange he would own this movie. It was apparently about relationships, and he was a bigger fan of action—or, embarrassingly, musicals, though occasionally he enjoyed an art-house flick so long as it was absurd and beautifully filmed.

It was only a few scenes in that Zach's body went slack. Leith held very still, listening to Zach breathing, slow and steady. With their heads so close, Leith could smell his shampoo and cologne, and a quick glance at Zach's face proved he was fast asleep.

When Zach shifted, moving so that his head rested on Leith's shoulder and his body went even more relaxed, any guilt Leith felt that he'd selfishly kept his exhausted friend from going home was instantly overridden by a rushing current of desire, and a thrill of peaceful rightness.

Leith nearly turned the movie off several times, but the idea of waking Zach with his movement always stopped him. Although it wasn't only for Zach's benefit. Every glance at

Zach's sweet, sleeping face threatened to overwhelm him, and his fattening cock and tingling nipples put to rest any doubts he'd tried to feed himself over the last few days about the reality of his attraction.

He wanted Zach, and he wanted him *badly*.

By forcing his eyes on the screen, Leith faced the growing realization that whoever he'd been before, he'd definitely been aware of his attraction to men. Watching the two boys on screen kiss while the man next to him snuggled closer until his head rested on Leith's chest was exciting in a way he'd never in his memory known with a woman—even in the midst of sex itself.

Leith's cock grew achingly hard, and he yearned to touch Zach's hair, to feel it feather between his fingers. He could feel his heartbeat pounding restlessly through him, beating in his cock, his nipples, and batting its wings against his throat.

Eventually he couldn't watch the movie anymore. Blind with desire, he wanted more than anything else in the world to roll Zach onto his back and rut against him until he came in his sweats. Reluctantly he disengaged himself from Zach and unplugged the DVD player before slipping into the bathroom.

In the darkness, Leith took hold of himself. Fantasy images flowed through him, strange and intimate: soft skin, and Zach's mouth on his cock—wet, wet, wet, and strong. God, so strong, sucking him and kissing him, and taking him into his throat…

Leith groaned and his dick swelled eagerly in his hand, the rush of blood and clenching need in his gut wrenching free a gasp. Moving his hand over his cock quickly now, he imagined Zach's tongue twisting over the head, sucking and taking him deep. He imagined Zach's hot green-blue eyes staring up at him as his mouth—his beautiful, rich mouth—distended around the shaft—

Leith grunted, humping the air as an orgasm ripped through him. He bit down on his lip, pleasure and relief releasing in his body with each spasm. When he could breathe again, he flipped on the light. The flood of brightness brought some semblance of sanity to him, and even though he was wrung out and shaky, the reality of come on his hand, the floor, and the underside of the sink captured his attention away from the compelling images of his fantasies.

After quickly cleaning up his mess, he bent to splash cold water on his face. Then he lifted his head to gaze into the eyes of a man who was absolutely, positively at least a little bit queer.

Zach was still asleep in Leith's bed, his clothes rumpled and his hair mussed. It was breathtaking. Leith swallowed hard, and as though of its own volition his hand reached out to touch. Zach stirred and opened his eyes, and Leith snatched his hand away.

"Hey," Zach mumbled.

"Sorry. I didn't mean to wake you."

"You okay?" He was clearly still mostly asleep and not aware of what he was saying.

"Yeah. Just tired."

Zach said, "Okay," and then turned onto his side and fell immediately back to sleep. Leith waited until he was sure that Zach would stay put before curling up in the fold-out soft chair. It wasn't bad, like Arthur had said. He watched Zach reach for the remaining pillow and clutch it tightly.

Leith pondered Zach's sleep-slack face. What if Zach knew how Leith had felt about him? What if he'd pitied him? Because surely if Zach cared about him, too, they would have been together? Wouldn't they have been more than just good friends?

Later Leith finally fell asleep counting Zach's beautiful, slow, and tender breaths.

THE NEXT MORNING
VLOG ENTRY #5

INT. BAR – BOOTH – DAY

Zach brushes a hand over his wet hair and smiles softly.

ZACH

Hello, darlings. Well, it was quite a night. No, not like that. I stayed to watch a movie with Leith, and ended up crashing for the whole night. Leith was a perfect gentleman and took the chair. Yes, I inadvertently kicked a head trauma patient out of his bed. Now I'm at work, and I'm the only one here so far except for Tony in the kitchen. I've got a ton of stuff to do, but all I want is to be with Leith.

He smiles more broadly and waves a hand at the camera.

So instead I'm talking about him with all of you. He's doing better, which is good.

Zach's smile fades.

He still doesn't remember me, for the record. It's like...I want to be with him every minute, but it hurts at the same time. Still, it doesn't matter how I feel. He needs me. I see it when I'm with him—the look in his eyes that tells me that some part of him recognizes that we click together.

There have been moments, small flashes, where...am I kidding myself? I don't think I am, I really don't, though I suppose you'll all tell me I am. But there's something there.

Sometimes he touches me, or we brush against each other, and there's this look on his face...and believe me, it's a look I know quite well. He *likes* touching me. A lot. And it surprises him, but he doesn't pull away. He was asking me questions about this gay movie, and I just couldn't answer. I'm afraid that if I let myself hope...

Zach sighs and shakes his head.

I can't help it. I have to have some hope. I love him, and I want whatever I can have of him. If I'm fooling myself, so be it. I'll take his friendship, and I'll give him everything I can for as long as he'll let me.

Don't get me wrong; it hurts to be around him, loving him and knowing he doesn't remember anything about who we were. But I can take it. I can do anything if it's for him.

Zach bites his lip. He runs his hands through his damp hair and takes a long, deep breath before continuing.

What I can't risk is losing him. Not right now. I'll keep what we were to myself for the time being. His doctor agrees with me, actually. Arthur and our friends understand that the doctor wants it this way for Leith at the moment, but I don't think they know all of this is also for me.

He lapses into silence for a few seconds.

If it has to come out—*when* it has to come out, and I know it will, then I'll deal with the fallout. I know when he leaves the hospital he'll have to know. Of course he has to know from me before he finds out from anyone else. But right now I can't handle it if he rejects me.

His face twists.

I remember how it was when he first felt attracted to me; how he was cruel at first in his refusal to accept his new understanding of himself. I can't handle him being cruel right now. I'm willing to risk putting it off another day or another year—whatever it takes to stay in his life. That's what I want to do.

Zach claps his hands lightly together, and leans forward.

I'd better get to work. I feel finally able to breathe a little again. Until next time, my loves.

Chapter Six

Have you ever been to India during monsoon season?" Dr. Thakur asked.

Leith peeled a petal off the rose he held and dropped it to the ground, shaking his head. "No. I've never been to India at all." Then he rolled his eyes at Dr. Thakur. "That I know of. Unless I've been in the last three years and no one has told me."

Dr. Thakur smiled. "No, as far as I know you weren't in India during any of your lost years. It wasn't a trick question."

Leith pulled a few more petals from the rose. He held them on his fingertips, examining the bright orange color at the middle of the petals, and the fuchsia on the ends.

"A few years back my wife, Bhavanha, wanted to return to India for her grandmother's funeral. It was the first time she'd been back since she was a small girl, and I attended the funeral with her."

Nodding, Leith brought the petals to his lips and blew, watching as they floated on the breeze and landed a few feet away in the gravel of the path.

"It was monsoon season, and so my introduction to India was, well, it was very wet."

Leith listened, but not very intently. He didn't know why Dr. Thakur was suddenly getting personal with him, but he supposed it was better than rehashing his own feelings again. It was getting very boring to say, over and over: *It's frustrating not to understand. It's confusing when I feel things that don't match my experience. It scares me when I'm in a situation and I can't be who I know the other person wants me to be.*

He hadn't told Dr. Thakur about the hard-ons he

consistently got around Zach, or the intense emotions Zach brought up in him. Both the thought of being with Zach and being without him made him tremble and ache. He still didn't know how to even begin to express those feelings.

"In the village where my wife's grandmother had died, there was a river, and it was wildly flooded by the monsoon waters. Every day this group of boys would trudge out in the mud and stand by the side of the river, pushing and shoving, and daring each other to go first."

Go first, Leith thought. Sometimes he felt torn into different people. One who wanted to hold back and wait—to not to push anything because the answers were surely coming. Another who wanted to tell the world to go fuck itself because he was starting a new life without any of the old hang-ups to deal with. And another who wanted to curl up on a bed with Zach and never leave. They all seemed to be playing a game of chicken with each other.

"Have you ever swum across a river?" Dr. Thakur asked.

"Sure," Leith answered. "Lots of times out camping."

"These boys, though, they weren't just swimming across a river. They were swimming across a *monsoon-flooded* river, with floating tree limbs, and debris rushing downstream. To make it across required daring, strong muscles, powerful lungs, a lot of endurance, and most importantly a ton of will-power and determination. And yet these young boys would jump in and risk it just for fun."

Leith could imagine it. It must be universal for young boys to egg each other on into doing something stupid.

"I was thinking about them this morning while reviewing your file. You have several options. You can leap back into whatever life you had before—go with the current, and wash out to wherever it is you end up. Or you can do something more than that. You can push yourself to find out who you are, no matter what memories you have or don't have. You can swim against the current until you reach the other side of the river."

Leith pondered it as he plucked another rose petal. Time was like a river, and memory was a current. Time flowed on without ceasing, no matter what or who tried to get in its way. But memory was changeable, and even losable. Like a current it could carry a person far away from their starting point, leaving them somewhere they might never have intended to be.

Like remembering how Zach's lips looked as soft as the rose petals Leith held on his fingertips, and that his eyes were sometimes as green as the leaves on the rosemary shrub filling the garden corner. Leith sighed deeply and dropped the petals. He didn't understand all this mooning over a guy, and yet he couldn't seem to make himself stop thinking about Zach, or to feel anything less than thrilled whenever Zach walked through the door.

"Leith? Are you still with me?"

He nodded.

"What I'm saying is that if a flood comes your way—a flood of anger, or of fear—don't let it carry you away. Fight that current and cross that river. Anyone can go with the flow. Be more than that. Challenge yourself."

"Okay," Leith said. "I'll try."

"Good. I'm glad to hear that." Dr. Thakur stood up and reached for Leith's hand. He allowed Dr. Thakur to pull him up to stand as well. "It's been a pleasure, Leith."

"I don't understand."

"I'll be referring your case to an outpatient counselor. Tomorrow you go home."

❀ ❀ ❀

Apparently I'll be facing a monsoon swollen river tomorrow.

Zach's immediate reply to Leith's text was a simple

question mark, and Leith thought about not telling him anything more. Just showing up at Blue Flight or the apartment and letting Zach be surprised. It was likely a bad idea.

I'm being discharged. Tomorrow I come home.

It took more than an hour for Zach to reply. Leith sat on the bench in the garden and stared at his phone, his stomach tied in knots.

Your room will be ready for you. See you then.

⧓ ⧓ ⧓

Leith carefully folded his shirts and placed them into the bag Arthur had brought. He was wearing his jeans and the blue polo Zach had bought him, and Leith's stomach flip-flopped at the idea that he was actually leaving. That he was going home to his own apartment—and Zach would be there.

He watched Arthur pacing the room, rolling and unrolling a newspaper, getting newsprint all over his hands. "Arthur," Leith said, smiling. "What's going on with you? Are you going to tell me before you rip that paper to shreds?"

Arthur tapped the paper against his palm. "I suppose I *should*. After all the doctor says I need to tell you before you find out for yourself."

Leith sat down on the side of the bed. "Okay, so tell me."

Arthur gave a tight, close-mouthed smile. "This newspaper is over a year old. I kept it because…well, isn't it always nice to see one's name in print?"

Arthur handed over the paper he'd been torturing, and Leith blinked at the gossip rag. On the cover was a blurry photo of him stepping into what looked like a boxing club. He read the headline aloud. "The Next Great Amateur?"

Arthur nodded and shrugged.

"So what is this? Some kind of story about me?"

"It's about you, and because of that it's about me…and

Mom and Dad. I want you to read it and then we need to talk about something else too."

"Is it a good article or a bad one? Why are you showing it to me now?"

Arthur made a face that seemed to indicate he felt the quality of the story was very much *meh* in his opinion. "Because this is the information that's out there about you, and everything in the article is true. You have a right to know it. Especially the less savory items, which are mostly about me I suppose, but it's a little bit about everyone."

Leith skimmed down looking for Arthur's name. "Are you fucking with me right now? You slept with women for money?"

"Oh yes, that. Well, it was years ago. When I first came to New York and had no income."

"I thought you got your start with what Mom left you."

"Come on, you know as well as I do there was barely enough there to last six months—much less the year it took me to get Joseph's Teeth up and going. And, for the sake of full disclosure, it was actually men I slept with for money. They pay more."

"*What?*"

"Yes, yes, so what? I'm sexually flexible. Ambi, omni, bi, queer—whatever it's called. Why call it anything? I don't see the point. Sex is sex. Leith, you used to know this, and you generally found it amusing."

"I did?" Leith scoffed. It didn't seem all that amusing to have his brother's humiliating personal business splashed across the front of a trashy newspaper.

"The important thing is that my current girlfriend's family knows about it all, too, and they've accepted it. Well, accept might be a strong word. It's more like they're resigned to it. Actually, they loathe me. Whatever. Miyoko and I have been able to work it out."

"So, let me get this straight, although I guess that's not the right word to use. You used to be a *male prostitute,* and now you're in a relationship with a woman I haven't met yet—or ever heard about—but you've sorted it all out?"

"Exactly."

"Why haven't I met this...what did you say her name was? Miyoko?"

"It wasn't serious until very recently, and you weren't really in a position to be meeting a lot of new people because you were so busy meeting old people."

"Arthur, what the fuck?"

"She's younger than me. Legal, though! She's legal!"

Leith stared at Arthur. "How legal?"

"She's twenty. Next month. Besides, it doesn't to me. The only people who really care are her parents." He sniffed and flicked his hair out of his face. "I'm ten years older than her and own a bar. Where she works. I'm not her parents' ideal, that's for certain."

"You're dating a nineteen-year-old employee. You're her *boss.*"

"You make it sound so tawdry. Zach's her boss too! Look, I didn't exactly plan this, but Miyoko's..." His gaze went distant, and he smiled softly. "She understands me. I always thought she was hot, but after your accident...she really helped me. We didn't even hook up for weeks—it was just...talking."

"Talking? It must be love then," Leith bit out.

"It's been stressful trying to make her parents understand my intentions toward Miyoko without seeming like even more of a...well, you know. But the heart wants what it wants. She wants me, and I want her. Her parents' disapproval of course means nothing to me."

"Of course."

Arthur sighed, his shoulders slumping.

"And this has been going on the whole time I've been here? Why you didn't mention it before?"

Arthur shrugged. "I didn't want to burden you. You've had your troubles. I've had mine."

"You say potato..." Leith said, shaking out the gossip rag again. His eyes took in the words, and as his brain supplied their meaning his stomach went cold and solid, like it was suddenly filled with stones. "Father addicted to gambling, and Wenz himself spent two years in prison for promoting an unlicensed boxing match and causing grievous bodily harm to a minor." *Two years in **prison**.*

Shame swept over Leith and he closed his eyes. "None of this is anyone's business but ours. This information is personal."

Arthur sighed and snatched the paper from Leith's hand. "It's all just *words*. What do they even mean in the end? I don't care."

Leith jumped up from the bed and grabbed it back. "You might not care, but I do." Of course Arthur had known he'd care. That was the reason he was telling him now instead of leaving it for him to discover later. Leith read further and scoffed. "'At the age of eleven the young boxer's mother killed herself?' Arthur, that's libel. That's an outright lie."

"Actually, Leith," Arthur began, gently.

No. Leith didn't want to hear it. He shoved his bag off of the hospital bed, his clothes and meager belongings spilling across the floor.

Leith shook the newspaper at Arthur and yelled, "That's a lie. Don't! Just shut up!"

"Leith, before...before the accident you already knew this. I told you when you got out of prison. Dad hadn't wanted you to know. You were so young when it happened. But after his death, I thought you had a right to know the truth."

"The *truth?*"

"She was depressive. It wasn't her fault."

Arthur had his hands up and a look on his face that made Leith want to punch him. It was a sympathetic, brotherly expression that made him nauseous, because if Arthur was looking at him like that, then it was true. Then his mother had actually—no, it was too much for him to imagine. He'd just been a kid—a little boy. *Why* would she do that? How could she do that to them?

As Leith started to pace by the bed, Arthur's voice came through the haze of building rage.

"It was pills. She left a note. They didn't kill her right away, but the damage was done, and her organs shut down."

Sweet Easter bread, and cool fingers on his forehead when he was sick. A new pink swirly dress that she'd worn while she danced and laughed with him in the street when he was ten, and purple flowers she'd saved in a vase until they were withered and brown because he'd picked them for her on his way back from school.

All of these things and more crested in his mind like a rushing wave, and he slammed his fist against the mattress. But it didn't hurt enough; it didn't make a dent.

"Leith, it's—"

Leith shoved Arthur, drawing his fist back to strike. "Shut up! You're lying! Don't say it again!"

The firm grip on his arm came out of nowhere, and Leith whirled around, his fist flying blindly. He registered Zach's face just as his knuckles connected, and the crack of fist on jawbone and teeth clattering together echoed in the room. Zach crashed to the floor, and Leith's stomach plummeted.

He dropped to his knees beside Zach immediately, reaching

out to him. "Zach, no. No, no, no. I didn't...no."

Zach held his hand against his chin, and his face was twisted with pain. But the worst was the expression in his eyes: fear. Leith crept back until he was pressed against the wall. He closed his eyes and waited. Nurses streamed in, and there was a great deal of animated talking and shuffling around. He couldn't look at Zach. He couldn't look at anyone.

"He's got quite a swing, doesn't he?" Arthur said.

Zach made a quiet, hurt sound, and Leith squeezed his eyes even tighter.

"Come on, Mr. Stephens," a nurse said. "Let's get some ice for that."

More footsteps came and went, and Leith covered his ears and pressed his eyes against his knees, trying to block out the world. Muffled though it was to his plugged up ears, the next voice he heard wasn't unexpected.

Calm as ever, Dr. Thakur said, "I'll handle this now, Mr. Wenz. Don't worry. Everything's going to be fine. Why don't you and Mr. Stephens leave the room now? I think your brother could use some space to breathe."

When Dr. Thakur knelt beside him, Leith opened his eyes. He saw Zach and Arthur being pressed through the doorway by a nurse. Both looked over their shoulders at him. Zach held an ice pack on his chin, and his eyes were greener and brighter than Leith had ever seen.

"We need to get you examined, Mr. Stephens," the nurse was saying.

Zach, supported on Arthur's arm, turned his back on Leith and left the room.

Dr. Thakur dismissed the other nurse and the security team. "He's not a danger. He calmed himself as soon as he realized what he'd done."

Leith covered his face with his hands. He breathed in and out, waiting like he'd learned to wait in prison, and tried to stop his body's shaking.

"Well, Leith, what do you make of this situation?" Dr. Thakur asked when they were alone.

Leith whispered, "I don't think I'm ready to go home."

"No, it looks as though you're not."

Dr. Thakur put a reassuring hand on his shoulder, and Leith bowed his head to cry.

🎀 🎀 🎀

Leith was drowning, fighting against a swift current, and he was never going to get his head above water. As soon as he could gulp a breath, he'd go under again, fighting hard to keep himself from throwing things, or punching the wall.

Zach, I'm so sorry.

His texts went unanswered.

In art therapy, he pounded the clay with all his strength, never bothering to attempt to mold anything out of it—just hammering it with his fists until the table shook, and the other patients stared at him with wide eyes. The counselor said nothing; she simply watched him with a bland expression that made Leith pound the clay even harder.

Please answer the phone, Zach. I don't know how else to reach you.

In between his regular therapy appointments, Leith haunted the hospital gym, running on the treadmill until he was blind with exhaustion. It still wasn't good enough. He nearly punched the blond trainer who tried to joke that Leith was in the gym so much now he should just set up camp by the treadmill. He'd had to close his eyes and throw some air punches while running just to get the urge under control. The trainer had the good sense to look nervous, and he hadn't spoken to Leith since.

I called Blue Flight. They said you weren't there, but I heard you in the background. Please call. I need to talk to you.

Dr. Thakur sat through two days of complete silence while Leith paced his office, and on the third day, he watched calmly as Leith trashed a bookshelf, yelling and throwing the books against the opposite wall. When Leith banged his fists against the wall for good measure before sliding down to the floor in a shaking heap, Dr. Thakur stood up from behind his desk and sat down next to him, saying nothing.

Zach, please call me.

In group therapy he listened to David Mueller suffer, again, through the realization that he couldn't make any new memories, and he sat through Jan Troxell reporting on the weather, again, and when it was his turn he stared at them all for a long time, feeling the words and rage welling inside.

He took some deep breaths, trying to hold it back, and he started out calmly enough. "What fucking good does any of this shit do me?"

He stood up then, his anger mounting. He said, pointing at Jan, "Her bullshit about the weather, and his endless moaning about his fucking memories, and no—don't tell me to stop, because he won't fucking remember that I've said this tomorrow, so what does it fucking matter?"

His hands were shaking. "How does this help me at all?" he yelled. "I've got a dead father, a mother who killed herself, and I'm missing three years of my fucking life. I'm in love with someone and I don't understand why! And my whore brother is fucking a girl who just stopped being a kid two years ago or some shit like that, and our dirty laundry is everyone's business! I don't want to box, but I want to box, and I hate that I don't remember almost winning, and I hate that I'm here, and I hate you for your stupid face, and I hate them for never getting better, and I hate all of this! All of it! Do you understand?"

The unruffled counselor regarded him evenly. "Thank you, Leith. I'm glad you shared that with us."

He turned around and punched the wall.

Zach, I don't blame you if you think I'm insane.

The guilt made Leith feel physically ill. Whenever he remembered the sound of his fist connecting with Zach's face, he nearly doubled over. Leith didn't know what to do. He needed to make it right. He was going to go insane if he didn't see Zach again, if only to tell him that he understood if Zach no longer wanted to be friends with a mad man. It wasn't as if Leith could blame him.

I understand if you can't talk to me right now, but just let me know that you're okay.

The texts still went unanswered. Leith typed in a final message, but he never pressed send. He kept it under drafts and looked at it several times a day, fingering the send button before turning his phone off and going to work out again. Even if he couldn't send the message, it somehow made Leith feel better just to see the words.

Zach, I don't understand it, but I think I'm in love with you.

༝ ༝ ༝

Stepping out into the garden, the heat was oppressive, and Leith stared up at a sky so bright it was almost white. He sat on his favorite bench where he often met with Dr. Thakur, shaded by the oak tree's branches. He picked at a loose thread on the seam of his jeans.

Burying his face in his hands, he remembered Zach's messed up hair when he'd spent the night, and the way Zach had smiled when Leith confessed his manly love of musicals, and the way Zach's hands moved when he talked like birds in flight, and how much Leith wanted to grab them and kiss them. Without Zach, he was floating away into despair and rage.

101

He didn't know how long he sat there. It was long enough for the sun to have poured heat into his bones, leaving him feeling exhausted and drowsy—so that at first he thought it was a dream.

"Hey."

Leith looked up slowly. It wasn't possible. Was it? He gripped the edge of the bench harder, and it felt very real. He stared at Zach standing there in the hospital garden. Zach's green T-shirt made his eyes seem even prettier, and his legs looked long and lean in dark jeans. A bruise still colored his chin, and Leith felt sick.

It wasn't a dream, and he didn't know what to say. "Zach," Leith began, and he lifted his hands and let them fall again. "I'm sorry."

"It wasn't your fault. I should have known not to get in the way of a fist like that."

Leith shook his head and kept his eyes averted, a lump forming in his throat and his eyes stinging. "Don't," he said. "Don't make it sound like that. It was me. I...ever since this accident, I just lose control. I'm not safe, I guess. Not safe to be around."

Zach knelt in front of him, sitting on his heels. "That's not true. You're going through a lot right now. You're scared, and you're trying to protect yourself."

Leith shook his head. "Please stop. I don't want to hear that."

"It's the truth, Leith."

"It's not!" Leith shrank back from Zach, frightened by his own outburst. He conceded, "Well, it's true, but it doesn't make it okay." He closed his eyes.

"Leith," Zach took his hand and squeezed it. "Please don't hide away from me."

Leith couldn't believe it. He opened his eyes and resisted the urge to jerk his hand away from Zach's grasp. "What about you? You didn't come back. You didn't take my calls or return my texts."

Zach took a slow breath and let it out. "I know. I'm sorry. *I was scared too.*"

Leith's throat was so tight, fighting back tears, that he could barely say, "I'm sorry." His chest ached with a pain so intense he thought he might die from it.

"No, no—not of you, Leith. Well...yes, I was scared of you, but not for the reason you think."

Leith stared at him. "Why then?"

"It's a secret, but I'll tell you if you promise to keep it to yourself, and you won't tell another soul?"

Leith nodded, his eyes locked onto Zach's. He wanted to do anything, any tiny thing to put this right.

"Sometimes I think if you really knew me, then you wouldn't like me anymore."

"Nothing would make me stop liking you."

Zach's eyes held his for a long moment. "I want to believe that."

"I don't know you. I don't even know why we're friends, and I still like you. I like you..." Leith swallowed hard and exhaled a shaky breath, searching for the right word. "Desperately."

Zach's eyes glowed.

Leith wanted to backtrack, erase and rewind, but instead he said, "I really need you around."

"Leith, I can be around for as long as you want." Zach reached up to Leith's face and stroked into his hair.

Leith's eyes fell to Zach's mouth, and when he flicked his gaze back to Zach's eyes, he was breathless to find an answering

103

tenderness there. When Zach rose up on his knees and gently kissed him, Leith felt himself loosen and unwind, awash with relief unlike any he'd known before. He kissed Zach back, amazed at Zach's lips, softer then the rose petals he'd held, and the strange scrape of stubble was shockingly tantalizing.

"Oh," Leith breathed against Zach's mouth.

"Shh," Zach said, and kissed him again.

Leith knotted his hands in Zach's shirt, dragging him closer between his legs, wanting more of his scent, and taste, and touch. Zach didn't resist, and Leith nearly cried in relief when Zach's hands tangled in his hair, pulling Leith even deeper into the kiss.

Leith gave himself up to the astonishing fact that although he was kissing a man, and his cock ached, hard and straining against his jeans, and though the air around him fairly hummed with his lust, he wasn't freaking out. Not even a little, and for the first time since he'd woken up in the hospital he felt completely at peace, like he was a river that had rushed home to the ocean, and found itself calm and still.

The next few minutes were a blur. Zach's hard shoulders felt right under his hands, and Zach's strong neck so good against his lips. He shivered at the scratch of barely there stubble against his tongue. They were strange sensations, entirely different from the bodies Leith was used to, and yet alive and vibrant, nearly quivering with life under his touch.

Leith ran his hands down Zach's arms, sturdy and well-built, muscled and beautiful, and he grabbed Zach's hands, moving one to the aching hardness where his cock pressed against his jeans.

Zach made a noise against Leith's mouth, and for a solitary second, Leith nearly woke from the lustful, deep trance he'd fallen into with a stab of worry that this was not what his friend wanted. But before he could speak, Zach's fingers outlined

Leith's cock, massaging the head and rubbing along the length. Leith spread his legs wider and dragged Zach closer still, Zach's mouth soft and wet, and eager against his own.

The friction along his cock was not nearly enough, and Leith pulled away from the kiss long enough to look into Zach's eyes, the brilliant green-blue nearly swallowed by lust-enlarged pupils. Leith whispered, "Zach..."

Zach took a deep breath, and his eyelashes fluttered as he seemed to try to calm himself. All the while his hand moved steadily over the denim covering Leith's cock. Zach glanced over his shoulder for a moment, and Leith remembered that an outside world existed and that they were in it.

He tore his gaze away from Zach's face, and his eyes traced over the patches of light and the red, orange, and pink roses; the thick of the shrub hiding them, and the oak tree that blocked the view the other direction. It wasn't entirely private, but he didn't care.

When he imagined stopping now, his cock throbbed and his heart pounded, and the depths of calm that seemed to fill him up threatened to ebb away. He couldn't let Zach move away from him now. He couldn't stop touching Zach's skin, or kissing his mouth, because there was no way he could handle going back to missing something—missing a piece of his puzzle. Missing *this*.

Zach's gentle eyes on his face seemed to track his thoughts, and he moved to unbutton Leith's jeans. His hand on Leith's cock was big and warm, and Leith shakily put his own over Zach's, feeling the tendons move as they jerked Leith's cock together. Disconnected thoughts flooded Leith's mind.

His hand is so big. His mouth is hot. How is this so good? I need this. So much. He's amazing.

And then, like a ribbon tying him to something he couldn't remember, he knew they'd done this before. He grabbed Zach's head, pulling him into another kiss, whimpering against Zach's

105

mouth as his hips lifted with small thrusts, pushing his cock into Zach's fist.

He rocked and gasped, and Zach broke free just as Leith clenched, feeling the intense grip of an intense orgasm begin. Zach ducked his head down, and his mouth was hot, hot, hot around the head of Leith's cock.

Leith hunched over him protectively, resting his forehead against the back of Zach's head. He grunted as Zach sucked, and shuddered hard as he came in a blinding rush, shaking and spurting into Zach's mouth. Zach swallowed before pulling off and carefully tucking Leith's cock back into his jeans.

The tenderness Leith felt for Zach could have brought tears to his eyes, but he pulled Zach up for another kiss, his own come tasting bitter and strange in Zach's mouth. Leith was filled with an emotion both new and all encompassing, spreading over him and leaving him exposed.

Zach's expression reflected an emotion even more delicate than his own, and Leith wanted to say something to make him smile, or make him understand, but he didn't know how to express it. Instead he found himself whispering, "Why didn't you tell me? I've been so unhappy."

Zach shook his head and brought his forehead to Leith's. "I'm sorry. I didn't want that. I didn't know what to do."

Then he dropped his face to Leith's shoulder and broke into soft tears. Leith didn't know what to do, so he went with his instinct and wrapped Zach in his arms, soothing him quietly in the oak's shade.

🎀 🎀 🎀

"Are you sure they don't mind if I stay all night?"

Leith waved his hand. "Of course not." He eyed the narrow bed, trying to breathe evenly. "They were fine with it last time, remember?"

He pulled back the covers and climbed in before Zach could raise any other objections about decorum. Besides, they were both in their underwear and there was nothing decorous about their obvious erections. If Zach was worried, he should get in the bed and cover up. He patted the mattress beside him, exhaling in a rush when Zach squeezed in.

"If you're sure."

"I'm sure." Leith didn't waste time getting Zach back in his arms, pulling Zach on top of him, chest to chest, their legs sliding together. The strength and warmth of Zach filled his senses, and he moved against him, shivering at the brush of leg hair against his own, the scratch of treasure trail, and the firm grasp of Zach's fingers where he held Leith's shoulders.

"Oh God," Zach murmured, his breath hot against Leith's cheek. "I've needed you so much."

"Shh, I'm right here." Leith slid his hand down Zach's back, gripping his ass and pulling his hips hard against his own, thrusting up so their cocks pressed together. "See? Right here with you."

Zach moaned, and Leith leaned in to press his lips against the soft skin at the base of Zach's neck, the skin he'd thought of so often. Heat coiled tight in his gut as Zach's pulse thudded against his mouth, and he breathed in the sweet, spicy scent of Zach's skin and hair. Zach trembled against him, and Leith held him closer.

He slid his tongue over the roughness of Zach's chin, thrilled with the bright catch of stubble—so male, so arousing, and so Zach. Leith roamed his hands eagerly, taking in planes of supple skin, the rough scratch of hair, and taut muscle. He couldn't get enough. It was so much...so much *sexier*.

Zach tangled his hands in Leith's hair, arching his back as soft, urgent noises tore from his throat. "Please touch me," Zach pleaded, his eyes closed and his hips moving urgently, his cock driving against Leith's as he squirmed under Leith's kisses and hands. "Please."

Leith was already touching him *everywhere,* and he spent a hazy moment confused by Zach's need. Then he understood. He rolled Zach over carefully, making sure to keep them both on the bed. "You want me to touch you?"

"God *yes,*" Zach said. "*Please.*"

Leith swallowed hard, trailing his hand over Zach's chest slowly and tweaking each nipple lightly, eliciting a soft bark of pleasure from Zach. He looked down to where Zach's cock strained against his underwear. *Oh God.* He hesitated, excitement and uncertainty tangling up in his gut. He'd never...not with another guy. He'd handled his own, but—

"Don't over think it," Zach said, touching Leith's face and bringing his gaze back to meet his own. "Just kiss me."

Leith lost himself in Zach's mouth, licking and sucking, tasting and being tasted, and as he did, he slid his hand under Zach's boxer briefs. He captured Zach's gasp when he took hold of his hot length and began to jerk him off just the way he'd always done himself.

The angle was of course different, and it made his mind spin a bit to think that he actually had another man's dick in his hand. But it felt so natural to have Zach throbbing in his grasp, flying apart under his touch. So powerful and right in a way he'd never experienced with women.

Zach moved against him, moaning into his mouth and bucking into his hand. When Leith sensed the change in his breathing and the tension in his body, he somehow knew it was time to pull back and *watch.* Zach in orgasm was stunning. His face crumpled and his mouth fell open. His body jerked and spasmed, and come splashed, white and compelling, against his pale skin.

"Leith!" he cried, his limbs twitching and his eyes rolling

back.

Leith didn't stop moving his hand until Zach reached down to stop him, his fingers trembling and his voice shaky as he whispered, "Enough. Please. Oh God, that was...yes, sweet Leith, that's enough now."

Leith didn't care if it made a mess—he grabbed hold of Zach and rutted against him, come smearing between their bodies as he kissed Zach's mouth, neck, shoulders, nipples—anywhere he could reach until he finally pressed his face into the softness of Zach's neck and came in his boxer briefs.

Zach rubbed a hand up and down his back, whispering, "I'm so happy. God, Leith. I've missed you so much."

Leith kissed him softly. He didn't know if it was possible, but he'd missed Zach too.

Later, after their shower and a change into fresh sleepwear, they cuddled in the narrow bed. Leith couldn't get over having made Zach come. The surreal familiarity and novelty all mixed up in a jumble.

"How did we get together?" he asked, rubbing his fingers over Zach's chin.

Zach shook his head and looked away.

"Did you...or did I? I mean, how did I know? You know, that I wanted you?"

Zach put his fingers on Leith's mouth, his eyes dark and wounded. "Let's just enjoy this, okay?"

Leith nodded, and they kissed on and off until Zach went down on him again and Leith forgot to be curious.

INT. APARTMENT – TABLE

Zach sits at the dining table in the apartment. The door leading to the hallway is open behind him, and his hair still wet from the shower. A bruise is visible on his jawline.

ZACH

Hello, my loves! I have amazing news. Amazing news! I know that you'll understand, my wonderful, super, fantastic followers, just how incredibly happy I am today.

Leith kissed me yesterday! Well, technically I kissed him. But! He was incredibly enthusiastic in his response, and then he asked me to stay with him in the hospital, and he was *very* persuasive.

He smiles and bounces in his seat.

And, in *even better* news, he's talking to the doctor this morning about coming home tomorrow. I can't wait to have him back here. I'm trying not to get my hopes up about this, but as you can see I'm failing miserably. It's possible I'll go back to the hospital tomorrow to pick him up and find that he's changed his mind. Or he'll be embarrassed and recalcitrant, but, as you can see—

He pushes his chair back and indicates his jiggling knees.

Yep, I'm failing at managing my emotions. He

kissed me! We made love. He held me and touched me, and it was just like—no, not just like before. It was different than before. He's different, but so much the same.

He sighs and shakes head.

I have to be careful. I can't allow myself to pretend or imagine for even a moment that Leith hasn't been changed by this experience. In some ways I feel like my Leith died, and this is a new one that I'm learning all over again.

Zach covers his mouth with his hand and his eyes grow large. He moves his hand away from his mouth and shudders.

I can't think of those things. I love him now and I loved him then, and I won't think about those things. It drags me under and I have to stay on top of the water. I have to keep swimming.

He claps his hands on his knees and lifts his chin.

I know it's been a while since I posted. I've been under a lot of stress, obviously, and I hope you'll forgive me.

Believe it or not, only four days ago I was sure I'd made a mistake with Leith. I thought it was going to be over between us. See, I interrupted an incident between Leith and his brother, and Leith accidentally hit me.

He waves a hand toward the bruise on his jaw.

111

Before you freak out, trust me that no one feels worse about this than Leith. He was devastated. And it wasn't so much that it made me question my resolve to always be there for Leith, but it did make me wonder if me being around was helping him at all. Or if once he knew the truth he'd be in an even worse place emotionally. He trusts me, and I worried if he found out I'd withheld such information about us, he'd lose that trust, and that would be it.

I admit I was scared too. I'd finally resigned myself to being his friend for as long as I could keep it that way. But then he was going to come home, and I knew I had to tell him the truth. That day I'd come to the hospital to tell him everything, and then...when I saw he was so vulnerable, and so easily wounded...I thought about taking the coward's way again.

I nearly bought another ticket to Italy but Marian and Ava talked me out of it. Still, I waited a few days before going to him because I had to resolve myself to telling him the truth. I was terrified. I should have at least answered his texts, but I was paralyzed. I can't even tell you how frightened I was. But then when I saw him...I didn't have to tell him anything. Somehow, we came together and he simply *knew*.

His face lights up.

Now he'll be home soon. It's like the world has

turned around completely. Yesterday I thought I might never see him again, and now I'm working out the details of a special surprise for him. In fact, I have to meet someone in ten minutes to finalize something. Oh wow, I'm running late. This took longer than I thought.

Dear viewers, thank you so much for the support you've given me. I know it's not over yet. I'm sure there will be more problems ahead, but I know I have friends I can count on, and that means a lot. Thank you.

More later! Perhaps I'll have Leith sitting next to me again the next time I post. You can meet him again. I think you'll like him.

Chapter Seven

Dr. Thakur nodded along as he wrote notes in Leith's file. "So, you feel much calmer now?"

"Yes," Leith said. "I think I'm ready to leave the hospital." He wanted to be near Zach. All day. Every day.

"And does this have anything to do with the sex you had with your friend Zach yesterday?"

Cheeks burning, Leith looked down at his knees and rubbed his hands against his pant legs. He didn't know what to say so he turned his attention to Dr. Thakur's bookcase, reading the titles for the hundredth time in the last week alone.

"The nurses were very amused," Dr. Thakur said. "Of course news of it would reach me."

The silence grew very long until he finally met Dr. Thakur's gaze and said, "It felt right. Really right."

Dr. Thakur nodded. "What did Zach tell you about before?"

Leith shrugged. "Nothing. He didn't want to talk about it. But somehow I know that we've done...*that* together before. I don't remember it, but I know. I just know."

"I see. Leith, I think you've probably realized something important. Your memories aren't gone, so much as inaccessible. The brain is a mysterious thing in many ways, and while you might not be able to consciously remember things from your past, there may be *unconscious* memories that defy a narrative explanation but still exist and motivate you nevertheless."

Leith nodded. He'd experienced that—the way he was pulled by strong currents of emotion or need that his conscious mind scrambled to make sense of. He came back to Dr. Thakur's question. "What do you know about Zach and me? From before?"

Dr. Thakur sighed and put down the file. He studied his nails for a moment. "Why do you ask?"

Leith thought it should be obvious. "Because it's my life, and I would like to know."

"It isn't just your life. You must realize that other people were affected by your injury, and it has been a constant balancing act to take the wishes of those people into account while also putting your emotional and psychological health first. I can tell you this, since you know it for yourself now: you were previously involved with Zachariah in a sexual and romantic way. Your friends and family were aware of your relationship. From all accounts, you were happy."

Jaw dropping, Leith stared at Dr. Thakur. Blood rushed in his ears. "You knew this. You knew all of this and you didn't tell me."

"Leith, it may be difficult for you to understand, but there are times when less information is the better route to take, especially when dealing with permanent memory loss. Imagine how your reaction to Zach might have been different had you been told immediately who he'd been to you. Now imagine how that reaction might have hurt him, and might have damaged you as well. My stance was that if the relationship and feelings had been erased, and if Zachariah didn't have the coping mechanisms at that time to deal with revealing your entire history to you, then it was better for the short term to let both of you heal as necessary. It appears your subconscious had plenty to say on the subject, and it led you back to where you most wanted to be."

Leith clenched his fingers into fists, a sense of betrayal rolling in his gut. "And what about Zach? Is this where he wants to be?"

Dr. Thakur shrugged. "I can only assume it is. He had the

115

option of moving on without you in his life, and it's clear he chose to accept you as you are now, in whatever capacity you were willing to be with him—even if that was just as a friend. Had he been angling for more, that could have been problematic, but the way he approached it seemed the healthiest for both of you. So I stood aside and let him choose how quickly he wanted to tell you about your relationship."

"And you get to determine that?" Leith asked, bitterly. "That's your job, is it?"

"It is." Dr. Thakur lifted an eyebrow and indicated Leith's fists. "Would you like to wreck a bookcase over it?"

Leith sat in silence for a long time, staring at the ceiling. Finally he said, "You should have told me."

"It's all a guessing game, Leith. I make choices and hope they are the right ones at the time, but there's no way to know. Perhaps I should have told you, or perhaps this ended up the best for everyone."

Dr. Thakur went to the bookshelf and pulled out a large piece of folded paper. He took it to his desk and unfolded it slowly, smoothing the edges down until it took up nearly his entire desk. "This is a map of the known universe. Or the known universe as it was about twenty years ago. It's an old map."

Leith didn't stand up but he could see the blue, black, and white arching over the paper.

"The sun, our sun, is ninety-three million miles away. Did you know that? It's not exactly right next door, and yet it is our neighbor." Dr. Thakur pointed along the edges of the map. "This is the outline of it, what astronomers call the 'observable' universe, because there is so much out there, so much that we can't understand, and they have to simply say, 'Beyond that, we just don't know.'"

Leith stood up to look at the map. The swirls of star clusters and planets were beautiful and compelling. He put his finger on

116

a galaxy and traced it.

"The mind is like this map, Leith. There is only so much of it we can understand. The rest of it? We have to say that we just don't know. I don't only work with the 'observable' mind. No, I have to take into account the billions and billions of things that make each person distinct—the cells and parts that make up *you*. The pieces, knowable and unknowable, that make you Leith and no one else, despite all you've lost. The universe doesn't stop being the universe at the edges of this map simply because we can't fathom it. It's still part of the whole, and you don't stop being Leith simply because you have lost some time and memories."

Dr. Thakur sat in his chair, his fingers continuing to run along the map, tracing out various star systems. "It's a universe of wonder and mystery, and a lot of us think that we're lost in it. I prefer to think that we're found. Do you understand, Leith? Sometimes the facts aren't what we need. Sometimes we need to be found in wonder."

Leith pondered it as he trailed his finger along the Milky Way.

Zach's face in orgasm and his hands on Leith's skin. His laugh when Leith accidentally tickled him. His eyes that were the same color as the little kinglet's feathers.

Not lost, but found. In wonder.

≈ ≈ ≈

His few items were packed up once again, and Leith sat on the edge of his bed, his leg jiggling up and down. He stared at his shoes and tried to stay calm. Zach's voice in the hall greeting the nurses brought his head up, and his heart seemed to swell while his palms broke out with sweat.

He suddenly worried that seeing Zach again would be awkward. That Zach would feel embarrassed at what they'd done together, and that whatever it was he felt wouldn't be returned. But when Zach opened the door, his eyes gleaming with a charming wickedness and his mouth twisted up in a happy smile, Leith's doubts dissolved. He ducked his head a little, embarrassed at just how happy it made him just to see Zach.

"Is everything ready to go?" Zach asked, clapping his hands together lightly before stepping between Leith's legs and wrapping his arms around Leith's neck.

Leith chuckled and grabbed Zach's hips to drag him closer, leaning in for a kiss. A sweet joy rose in him as Zach's lips met his, and he wrapped his legs around Zach's to trap him. "Now I have you," he teased, kissing Zach's chin. "And you'll never get free."

"Oooh, is that a promise?" Zach laughed and pressed his forehead to Leith's. Still smiling, he kissed Leith's mouth.

Leith fell back on the bed, dragging Zach on top of him, grabbing his ass and grinding his own hips up. He groaned and rolled Zach over, pressing a leg between Zach's and pushing his already hard cock down against Zach's thigh. His mouth never left Zach's lips or skin.

"Ahem." Arthur's voice cut through.

Leith's heart thumped, and an instinctive fear that his brother would be angry with him for kissing a guy kicked in. He rolled off Zach, tugging at his shirt to cover his erection. He reminded himself that Arthur had been with men, but he still held his breath.

"The nurses would certainly enjoy the show, but I believe they've kicked you out of this place, little brother. So, come on lovers, get yourselves together. Surely it can wait a few minutes."

Leith exhaled, embarrassment replacing the fear.

"Oh you're one to talk," Zach said as he sat and patted at

118

where his hair stuck up in a few places. "With all of the complaints I get from staff who walk in on you and Miyoko, someone might think you staged public make-out sessions because you get off on being seen."

"Ha," Arthur replied, his face reflecting his sarcasm. "I'd hate for the prudes to have nothing to clutch their pearls over. They live for the drama. The car is waiting. Do you have everything? Leith?"

Leith cleared his throat, his face hot. "Yeah, sure. Let me just..." He stood and turned his back to his brother, unzipping his bag and pretending to shift some stuff around, willing his dick to calm down.

Soon he was in the front seat of Arthur's car, silent in the face of the traffic, the skyscrapers, and the thousands of people on the sidewalks. He peered in wonder at the vibrant blue skies, glimpses of green grass in the parks, and the flash of the Hudson between the buildings and under the bridge. Before prison he'd only been to New York City a few times, and it felt new.

"This is where you like to go for runs," Zach said. "I'll show you the path you like best if you want."

"Sure." Leith stared at the expanse of the park.

A little later Arthur said, "That's the boxing club where you trained."

Leith turned his head to look more intently at the boxing club as they drove by. It didn't look like anything special, and he felt nothing at all about it. He looked at his hands, clenched them into fists, and tried to imagine being in the ring, fighting. He itched to hit a bag, or to feel the jolt of a punch landing on flesh, satisfying and solid. He nodded a little and closed his eyes. Yes, he thought that was something he wanted to do again.

When he opened his eyes next, the car was stopping in front of a building with a blue and green sign proclaiming that they'd reached Blue Flight.

119

"Our apartment is just above it," Zach said.

Leith stared at the building, searching for some kind of reaction, a feeling or a thought, but there was nothing. He didn't know why, but he was disappointed. He hadn't realized he'd been holding out the hope that he would still remember *something*. Dr. Thakur's voice came to him.

"Why does it matter?"

His only answer was Zach. Some part of him knew that he wanted to remember for Zach, and for whatever part of his subconscious that still understood what they'd been before.

"Leith?" Zach's voice from the back seat was a little worried, and Leith shook himself and smiled.

"Sure, sorry. I—I don't remember the place." He started to open the door, but Zach put a hand on his arm.

"Wait—we're not getting out here."

"Why not?" Leith asked. He wanted to get inside to face the apartment, and the people, and just get it over with. He hoped they hadn't planned a celebration, but something about Zach told him that he shouldn't be surprised if they had.

"I have a surprise for you," Zach said.

"A surprise?" Leith was confused. Didn't a surprise party lose its effect if the person was told beforehand to expect one?

"Yes," Arthur said, turning the car off and handing the keys over his shoulder to Zach. "Zach and his plans—"

"Uh-uh," Zach said, grabbing the keys. "None of that."

Arthur smirked a little and then said, "Have fun, little brother. I'll see you in a few days."

"A few days?" Leith asked, helplessly. As Zach crawled into the front seat and Arthur slammed the door shut, waving to them as he crossed in front of the car, Leith rubbed his face. "Where are we going?"

"Away. Someplace where the eager but annoying masses of

friends and family will leave you alone for a while, and I can have you all to myself. A quiet place in the woods. A cabin."

Leith didn't know what to say. Part of him was glad, excited even, to get back to nature. The woods had always been healing to him, but another part of him was frustrated. He'd been ready to dive in—tear off the Band-Aid and get the hardest part over with. His mixed feelings must have shown, because Zach put one hand on Leith's knee and turned Leith's face to him with the other.

"I think this will be best for you, Leith. You've been through so much. You need some time to cope. We both do. But if you don't want to go, of course we don't have to."

Leith looked in Zach's eyes, so sincere and persuasive, and he said, "Sure. It sounds great. I haven't been to the woods since before prison."

Zach's eyes darkened, and he turned away from Leith, fumbling with the keys as he started the car. "Well, it's about time then."

Leith nearly strangled on the sigh he held in, not wanting Zach to know that he'd seen his pain, Not wanting to admit to himself that he *had* been to the woods more recently than two years ago, and that memory was of course lost with all the others.

For just a moment or two he wanted to pretend that this was all there was. That they were going to the woods together for the first time, and it was new—something sweet and precious—for them both.

EARLIER THAT MORNING
VLOG ENTRY #7

INT. APARTMENT – COUCH
Zach perches on the edge of the cushions, grinning.

ZACH

Hello, my darlings! Thank you for the flood of comments and emails. I appreciate your support more than I could ever tell you.

I just wanted to let you know that Leith is indeed being released today. Operation Surprise Getaway is in full effect. I need to finish packing since we're headed to the wilderness. Well, it's a cabin with electricity and running water, so don't let me make it sound like we're truly roughing it.

But there's no wifi. Not even a phone line, and the nearest cell tower is not near enough. So I'll be going incommunicado for a few days, and I didn't want to worry you. Leith and I really going to be alone for the first time since this whole mess started, and...

He sighs and runs a hand through his hair.

I'm nervous as hell. Everything went so well yesterday. Kissing him again...touching him again...it's incredible. But now he's leaving the hospital, and we're going to be back in the real world. And maybe part of my reason for taking him away is that I'm afraid of what will happen once reality sinks in.

Will he still want me once he's out in the real world? Right now he barely knows anyone. What if he meets someone else? What if he likes him— or *her*—more than me? He said he was straight when he came out of the coma. Am I just an exception? Nothing more than muscle memory?

He takes a deep breath and blows it out.

No. I don't think I am. Before the accident, Leith had come to terms with his sexuality. He's not straight. And I have to believe that what he feels for me now is real, and not just some...echo.

He's silent for a few moments, his gaze distant. Then he shakes his head and claps his hands.

Sorry, I left the building there for a second. Okay, I'd better get moving. Leith's waiting. Catch you on the flipside, darlings.

He salutes the camera.

Chapter Eight

Forty minutes outside the city, the countryside sped by in a blur of green, blue, and yellow, with a hint of brown and gray now and again. They'd driven in silence for a long time, until Leith turned on the radio. He tried to stop on a station playing showtunes, but Zach pushed his hand away from the dial.

"Oh no you don't. Never again. I already suffered through one trip like that."

Leith said nothing, but he wondered if Zach was also allowing himself a moment to pretend that things were different—to believe even for a second that Leith remembered. Leith let Zach pick a top forty station.

The cabin was small and situated on a small glimmering lake. The view of the mountains was stunning. Leith stood by the car, leaning against it as he took long, deep breaths. He stared at the green trees around him, so lush in their late summer glory, and the source of the sweet, new air that he took into his lungs.

"Well?" Zach asked, pulling their bags from the car.

Smiling, Leith spread his arms wide. "It's amazing. I feel like I could fly right up into the sky."

Zach dropped the bags and grabbed him around the waist. "Sorry, but I can't allow that. You have to stay earthbound. With me."

Leith wrapped his arms around Zach and tucked his face against Zach's neck, breathing in his scent. He rested his chin on Zach's shoulder and whispered, "How is this happening? How is it possible? How can I feel these things for you? You're a stranger to me, yet I'm so…happy."

Zach sighed and turned his face to Leith's neck. His eyelashes fluttered against Leith's skin, giving him goose bumps. Leith rested against the side of the car, his eyes on the mountains against the sky, and his arms around Zach's shoulders, feeling the hard, strong line of where their bodies touched.

While Zach unpacked their groceries, Leith stood in the doorway of the cabin, Leith watching the shimmer of light on the lake. There was something about Zach's busyness that made Leith feel safe, as though simply by moving in the world Zach took charge of it, and made everything somehow easier.

Zach glanced up at Leith, and his eyes narrowed a bit. He scolded, "You could help out a little. From what I understand you lost a few years and some fine motor skills, but you can probably still figure out how to unload the groceries."

Leith shrugged, trying not to smile. "I like the view."

Zach waggled his brows suggestively and bent over to put some things in the bottom of the refrigerator. "This view? Or the one out the door?"

Leith swallowed as he got hot and flustered. He grinned and ducked his head, getting a better look at Zach's ass. It was the first sexual overture Zach had made since they'd kissed on the bed that morning, and Leith found himself feeling suddenly shy, like an inexperienced teenager who didn't even know where to start. But who was he kidding? He *wasn't* that experienced—not anymore.

When Zach stood and turned to face Leith he leaned against the kitchen counter and said with quiet speculation, "You always did like to make me come to you."

Leith didn't know what to say, but Zach's words felt like a challenge. He took a step forward, leaving the door open behind him. Zach's smile and tender expression were like a reward for his effort, and he stayed on course. Leith pressed him back against the counter. "Is this close enough?"

125

Zach laughed, his gaze flicking down to Leith's mouth. "What do you think?"

The kiss was hot. He lifted Zach onto the counter, dragging his hips forward until he could grind against Zach's crotch. Leith's physical reaction was immediate, and he found himself riding the accompanying waves of affection and lust with very little grace at all. His mouth dragged down the side of Zach's neck, seeking the soft spot he'd found so intriguing. When Zach gasped and shuddered in his arms, he grinned, tightening his hold.

"Leith," Zach said, pushing at him. "There's a bed."

"It's far away."

Zach laughed. "It's less than ten yards."

Leith considered. The counter was hard, and the bed would be soft. Zach wasn't going anywhere—he could have him in his arms again in only moments, and it would be better on the bed. They could take longer, and—yeah. The bed. It was a good idea. Zach was full of good ideas. He thought he must have loved Zach for having so many amazingly good ideas.

The path to the bed was slow, because he had to take off Zach's clothes, and his own shirt was left on the kitchen floor, and his jeans by the bedroom door, and then he'd had to stop and examine Zach's body in the light from the window, exploring the curve of muscle and dent of bone with his mouth, leaving wet spots that shined in the sun. Zach clung to him, his expression a mix of amazed tenderness and underlying surprise, like he nearly didn't believe what was happening.

Leith could barely believe it either, but it seemed that bodies had their own memory, because his fingers found the exact places that made Zach go weak, and his nose and mouth seemed to recognize the taste and smell of Zach's skin, making his heart thud and his cock jerk.

By the bed they rubbed their cocks together through their

126

boxers, and Leith grabbed Zach's ass to grind their hips together, loving the startling hardness pressed against his own. He shook his head, his breath shaking and labored, confused and turned on by the battling feelings of newness and familiarity.

The fall to the bed was fast, and Leith rolled Zach onto his back, looking down into his face and laughing softly. "This is crazy."

Zach's face seemed to shutter a little and Leith wanted it open again, open like it had been when Leith had kissed his shoulders and chest in the sunlight. "Zach..." He didn't know what to say, but Zach seemed to know, and he brought Leith down for another kiss.

Zach pushed Leith onto his back, and Leith gasped as Zach mouthed his way over Leith's chest, sucking and biting his nipples gently, making Leith arch up and grab hold of Zach's head. His stomach muscles tensed and his legs began to shake as Zach moved down, kissing toward his cock.

Leith's hands fell to the curve of Zach's neck as Zach bent over, and Leith shuddered at Zach's hot breath. Then it was Zach's hair under his fingers, and his hot, hot, hot mouth on his cock. Leith wanted to watch, but it was too good, and his head fell back on the pillow, his eyes shut.

He whimpered as Zach pulled off, and the rush of air against his cock felt shockingly cool. Leith pulled Zach up, kissing him and dragging his body onto his, thrusting his wet cock alongside Zach's. The scratch of their pubic hair and the drag of skin wasn't enough, but still so incredibly good.

Leith didn't know if there were words to describe how he felt—how his skin tingled and burned, nearly aching with want, or how his heart hurt with emotions that confused him and compelled him. It all drove him to want to consume Zach in every way—to please him and penetrate him, and somehow break it all down into the truth that his body knew and his mind denied him.

Zach's hands were on his face, and Leith opened his eyes to gaze up to Zach's, and he groaned at the heat and lust he saw there. Zach's answering smile made Leith push him over, instinctively hooking Zach's legs over his shoulders as he covered him, and he angled his hips so his cock dragged over Zach's ass, making a clumsy stab toward his hole.

Zach pushed against him as Leith kissed his neck, saying, "Wait, wait...hold on."

Leith steadied himself and backed off, watching as Zach rolled away.

"Let me just get—" Zach muttered. "Hold on. Don't go anywhere."

Laughing, Leith shook his head. He wasn't going *anywhere*, unless it was to drag Zach back to where he belonged— underneath Leith and grinding against him.

Zach dug around in a bag and came back with a condom and lube. Leith pulled him down, kissing his mouth, tasting his tongue, and holding him tight enough that it might have hurt, but Zach didn't complain.

The scratch of the edge of the condom wrapper against his arm brought Leith back to the plan, and he tried to take it from Zach's hand. But Zach broke free from their kiss and slid down Leith's body. Leith had a hard time not bucking his hips to thrust his cock toward Zach's mouth again. The condom felt cool as Zach slid it on Leith's aching cock, and he was breathless when Zach added lube to his entire shaft.

Then Zach knelt over him. "Leith, could you hold it for me?"

Leith nodded, his hand shaking as he gripped the base, the ridge of the lubed condom slick against his palm. He aimed it up.

Zach knelt there a moment, and Leith gazed at him—the lean muscles of his arms and chest, the dark thatch of pubic hair, and the hard cock sticking straight up, strangely pretty, with a small glistening smear of pre-come at the tip. Leith remembered the length of it in his hand the night in the hospital, and he wanted to lean forward and lick it.

He pushed up to do just that, but Zach pressed him back, leaning forward, his elbows on either side of Leith's face.

"Is this okay? Is this good?" Zach whispered.

Leith blinked up at him, unable to even process that Zach was asking him a question, every fiber of him was focused on somehow getting more. He wanted more of Zach's cock, more of Zach's ass, and more of Zach's mouth, so he kissed him and ran his hands up Zach's thighs, hoping Zach would understand his answer.

The press into Zach's ass took his breath away. It was so tight and hot, and he'd never felt anything like it. He moaned and bit his lip, trying not to shove up for more, letting Zach sink down on him slowly in small hunching movements that made Leith grip Zach's hips. He shuddered, his balls already drawn tight and his cock jerking.

He realized he'd closed his eyes, so he opened them, wanting to see Zach's expression, and it was amazing. Zach's mouth was open, his eyes far away and yet focused on Leith's face, and the soft look of lust and pleasure made Leith's hips buck up.

Zach gasped, pushing down until Leith was all the way in. His instinct was to move, to roll Zach onto his back, and fuck him hard, but he held very still, letting himself take in the sensations—Zach's pulse thudding against his cock in a steady but frantic rhythm; the hot, velvet sensation of his ass, and the grip of his anus around the base of Leith's cock, squeezing him.

"Is it good?" Zach asked.

Leith growled and pulled Zach's head down, kissing him and sucking on his lips, as he thrust up, driving into Zach's ass.

Zach's hands were in his hair, and they rocked together hard and fast until Leith couldn't fight it anymore, and rolled Zach onto his back. He needed to be in control. Wanted to be on top of Zach, protecting him, fucking him, holding him open, and driving into him. It all felt so natural, so right to be doing this with a man—with Zach.

Zach's eyes were closed and his head thrown back as Leith fucked him, and Leith greedily looked down at where his cock was sliding in, loving the tight grip and incredibly turned on by the way Zach's ass seemed to cling to him as he pulled out. Zach's noises were incredible, and Leith wanted to bottle them and own them, and never let anyone else hear them. They were so intimate and wild, and the small whimpers and pleas drove him on.

Zach's hands gripped Leith's forearms, and his legs shook on Leith's shoulders. Leith licked his lips, looking down at Zach's cock as it bobbed between them, the tip of it slick with pre-come, and a trail of it through the dark hair under his belly button. Leith wanted to taste it, but he didn't want to stop fucking Zach, so he let go of Zach's leg and ran a finger over the tip of Zach's cock, bringing it to his mouth to lick.

Zach's eyes went smoldering and dark, and he whispered something that Leith didn't hear over the slap of their skin together. The taste was familiar and right. Leith licked his palm and took Zach's cock in his hand, jerking him in time to his thrusts. Zach threw his head back and seemed lost, his hips bucking up, and the low, wild noises building in his throat and gaining pitch as Leith continued to increase momentum.

"Leith," Zach moaned.

Leith bent down, sucking one of Zach's nipples into his mouth, shuddering when Zach bucked up and cried out, and hot, wet come shot all over Leith's chest. Leith gasped at the tight clench of Zach's ass, and he lunged to kiss Zach's neck as he rode Zach through the aftershocks of orgasm. He continued to thrust as Zach caressed his back.

He whispered into Leith's ear, "I love you."

Shaking and trembling, Leith took a deep breath, smelling Zach's cologne, and shampoo, and the fresh air from outside, and the familiar scent of Zach's come. He slammed into orgasm, whimpering and spending load after load as his mind exploded with all of the stars of the observable universe.

🎀 🎀 🎀

Zach's head rested on his chest, and Leith ran his fingers lightly through Zach's hair. The sex had been good, no it had been incredible, and he almost felt as though he'd never had sex before, because if it was supposed to be like that…well, it hadn't. He wanted to laugh, and he wanted to thank Zach, but he didn't know just what to say that wouldn't seem odd. Especially since for Zach this wasn't the first time they'd done this.

That thought made Leith uncomfortable, and he shifted restlessly, surprised to find himself asking, "Was it always like that with us?"

"Yes," Zach mumbled.

"From the beginning?"

"Every time, pretty much. You always make things ridiculously intense." He kissed Leith's flushed chest. "Not that I'm complaining."

Leith was quiet, a pit of anger growing in his stomach in the blink of an eye. He sat up, dislodging Zach from his chest. He huddled with his back to Zach, but he could feel him there, over his shoulder, sitting in the midst of the wrecked sheets, scared, hurt, and confused.

"Do you need to…be alone?" Zach asked, his voice high

and tight.

Leith shook his head, wanting to turn around and take Zach into his arms, but wrestling with a sudden rage he had a hard time expressing.

How could he say he was jealous of himself? How could he explain that he hated that someone else—that another version of *him*, one he didn't remember—had heard Zach's noises. Had felt him come around his cock, and had kissed him for long minutes afterwards. It made no sense, but he wanted to crush the other Leith. To make it so he'd never existed.

"Okay, so last time…the first time we had anal sex, you did freak out a little bit," Zach said, anxiously.

Leith snapped, "I'm not freaking out. And I don't want to hear about him."

"Who?"

"Me." Leith shut his eyes, trying to get his emotions under control.

Zach made an even stranger noise, and Leith heard the sheets rustling, and then felt Zach's arms around him. His chin nestled against Leith's shoulder.

Leith looked down at him, and he couldn't help but smile a little at Zach's big, worried eyes. "I'm not crazy, okay?" Leith said, and then scoffed. "Okay, well, maybe a little crazy. Jealous of myself." He laughed. "That's not normal, is it?"

"Last time I checked, this was not a normal situation," Zach said. "And I'd tell you there was nothing to be jealous of, but it was you, and you're amazing, both now and before, and…" Zach stopped, and shook his head, closing his eyes. "I don't want to think about before either. Let's be here now. We need to move forward. Before doesn't matter. We don't need to talk about it."

Leith didn't know if he agreed, but seeing the hurt flashing over Zach's face, and hearing the weird tightness in his voice, he didn't want to argue. Not now when he was still trying to face the fact that he'd nearly had to find a way to beat himself up to satisfy his jealousy. He didn't think a fist in the mirror was a good way to start their time alone together.

Leith dreamed he was having sex with Zach in an old, junked car while his first girlfriend and his mother watched from behind the bars of a prison cell. He tried to tell Zach that they should stop having sex, that they were being watched, but he kept forgetting and he'd find himself still going at it despite his humiliation and anxiety.

It'd been a horrible dream, and he woke up alone in the cabin's bedroom, the late afternoon sun spilling through the window. As he studied the dust motes circling in the air, he wondered what Dr. Thakur would make of the dream, though Leith knew he would have never told the doctor about it.

He stretched and shook away his nerves, listening for Zach but hearing nothing. He pulled on his jeans and a T-shirt, and padded barefoot out to the kitchen and living room, but Zach wasn't in the cabin at all. Leith could see him out by the lake, standing with his hands in his pockets and his shoulders hunched, staring out at the water or the mountains.

Leith stood at the window, wanting to go out and join him, but there seemed to be something incredibly private about the moment. He didn't want to interrupt.

Eventually Zach turned to the cabin and slowly trudged up toward the door, pausing by the fire pit to kick at the bricks laid out around the edges. Rubbing a hand over his face, he seemed to shake something off. Then he faced the door with an expression of determination that made Leith's heart clench and ache. He didn't want it to look like he'd been spying on Zach, so he turned his back to the window and leaned against the counter, trying for nonchalance but feeling knotted up inside.

"Hey, you're awake," Zach said, his voice cheerful and light. "Are you hungry? You didn't have a warm meal at the hospital. Are you up for one now?"

Leith forced a smile and turned. "Sure. I'll start cooking."

"You do remember how to cook don't you?" Zach asked, approaching with a smile and grabbing Leith's shirt playfully. "And I do mean cook—not that thing you do where you heat something up from a can and call it food."

Leith swallowed and nodded. "Yeah, sure. My mother taught me..." and he trailed off, remembering that his mother had *killed herself*. That she'd taken pills and removed herself willingly from his life. He cleared his throat, looking away.

"Hey," Zach said, gently. "You're tense. Did you sleep okay? It seemed like you needed a nap."

"It was just a bad dream, I guess." He shrugged off the melancholy image of Zach by the lake and pushed back his thoughts of his mother. "I'm fine. I should get started."

But Zach didn't back away, and he took Leith's face in his hands, gazing into his eyes before kissing him. "It's good that we came here. You're already overwhelmed and it's just us. There would be too many people back at the apartment."

Leith nodded and leaned into Zach's touches, closing his eyes and letting the soft caress into his hair relax him. He remembered Zach's expressions as he'd fucked him, and the noises he'd made when he came, and he opened his eyes, feeling hot and hungry.

Zach smiled and kissed his lips, murmuring, "Let's eat. We have all night, and tomorrow, and the next day."

Leith angled Zach back against the counter and kissed him again, keeping his eyes open, watching Zach's face, looking for some assurance that it was really him that Zach was kissing. Zach pulled away, though, laughing and slapping his ass. "Come on, I need to eat."

Leith let him go.

Zach looked over his shoulder as he bent to get stuff out of the fridge, his face lined with concern. "Leith?"

"Yeah, sorry." Leith opened drawers, looking for knives to chop the vegetables that Zach was laying out on the counter. He found one that seemed halfway suitable and grabbed the large squash first, carving into the side of it the way he'd carved pumpkins as a kid, his hands clumsy and rough.

Zach watched for a few moments. "Do you want me to finish it?"

"I can do it," Leith said, nearly slicing his thumb. "It's going to take time." He rolled his eyes. "And practice. Or that's what they tell me." He didn't mention to Zach how strange it was to see his handwriting come out in strange, crumpled block letters like a kindergartener.

Zach watched in silence for a few more minutes, and then burst into action, opening a bottle of sparkling water, setting the table, starting the water boiling on the small stove.

Once the meal was cooking, Leith took his glass of sparkling water outside and stood in the dusky light as evening fell. Zach sat on the stoop of the cabin, resting his head against the doorframe, sipping his drink and looking relaxed.

After a moment of contemplation, Leith walked down to the side of the lake, pulled off his boots and socks, and rolled up his jeans. The water was cold, and he kicked at it with his toes. He raised his arms and let them fall, feeling the immensity of the space all around him—the eternity of the sky above, the vast distance to the mountains, and the wet expanse of water.

A deep breath in, and he let it out. Another, and he threw his head back, yelling, feeling and hearing it echoing all around.

A blur in his peripheral vision was his only warning before Zach leaped onto his back and toppled them both into the water, splashing and laughing—and cursing at the cold. Leith grabbed Zach and tickled him, and then pushed him into the water before Zach lunged, shoving him back.

The dreck at the lake bottom slipped beneath Leith's hands and feet, and he nearly went under. But he gained his footing and tripped Zach, who was trying to escape the lake. When Zach came up again sputtering, Leith kissed him, the water tasting earthy and tangy on his lips.

Dinner had to wait for another shower, and the blow job Zach offered, and when they sat down with their plates of overcooked food, the stars had come out. They ate on the floor in front of the fireplace, wearing nothing but their boxers. Zach lit a few citronella candles to keep the bugs away, and they flickered and guttered in the breeze from the screen door.

Pushing his empty plate aside, Leith crawled over to Zach, settling down with his head in Zach's lap. He closed his eyes and rested, listening to Zach eat a few more bites of dinner.

When Zach put his plate on the floor, Leith turned his head to nuzzle at the opening in Zach's boxers, smelling the musky scent of his pubic hair.

Zach's hands fell into his hair, and Leith felt an instinctive urge to pull Zach's cock out and suck it. He wondered at the intensity of this desire, and he sat with it a moment, feeling Zach's fingers playing in his hair, and the insistent press of Zach's cock against his cheek His heart rate responded, and a curl of nerves and lust unfurled in his stomach.

He'd done it before, he knew that he had, but he had no memory of it. Could he live up to what Zach expected? Would he know what to do like he had in the bedroom? Why was he thinking about it instead of just doing it? His own cock was growing heavy, too, and he wanted to get his mouth on Zach's

136

because he knew if he could just forget—just give up his worries—he'd love it.

He closed his eyes, and took several slow breaths. Then he kneeled, reached into Zach's boxers, and pulled out Zach's hot, smooth cock. He studied it in his hand, pretty and a dusky pink, the head brighter than the rest, and he pulled the foreskin up and down a little, watching Zach's hips respond. Then he looked into Zach's eyes, and laughing a little at the hot desire there, asked, "Do you like this?"

Zach nodded, swallowing hard. "I like everything with you."

Leith's heart was open and vulnerable, and he knew his face reflected it. "I don't know how to... Not anymore."

Zach's eyes grew tender, and he caressed Leith's cheek. "I'll love whatever you do."

Leith quirked a brow and gently gnashed his teeth, pretending to bite.

Zach chuckled. "Oooh, you're so funny, aren't you now?"

Leith laughed, relaxing and kissing Zach's cheek, the stubble scratching against his lips. He ducked down between Zach's legs, bringing his lips to the tip of Zach's cock. He kissed it lightly, noting the soft, delicate feel of the skin. He closed his eyes and opened his mouth, taking Zach's cock in and sucking.

And just like before, it was easy—it was like he'd done it a million times, and yet it was all new: the way Zach's hips lifted and sought more, the bitter taste of Zach's pre-come coating his tongue, and the scratch of pubic hair against his nose and fist as he jerked the base of Zach's cock along with his rhythmic sucking.

Zach's noises from above were soft and high-pitched, somewhat different from the deeper noises he'd made when Leith fucked him. More delicate somehow, and needy. His hands in Leith's hair were gentle, and Leith remembered how he'd grabbed Zach's head in the shower. He wanted to make Zach lose control like that too.

He increased the suction and twisted his tongue in Zach's slit on the upstroke, and Zach's hands gripped his hair hard. Leith hummed happily, and Zach whimpered, his hips stuttering and his stomach clenching and unclenching against Leith's cheek.

"Leith," Zach said, his voice breathy. "Just like that."

Leith twisted his tongue on every stroke, and Zach hunched over him, his hips twitching. Zach made hot sounds that left Leith quivering, and he reached down to stroke his own cock as he sucked Zach's. Leith knew even before Zach started to shake and say his name over and over that Zach was going to come.

Zach's cock swelled a little in his mouth, the skin growing tighter, and Leith pulled up to the head when the spurts began. Zach jerked, and his hands in Leith's hair tugged hard enough that it hurt. Zach's orgasm was short, but hard, and when Leith pulled off, swallowing the bitter come and wiping his mouth with the back of his hand, Zach's eyes sparkled with what looked like tears.

Leith touched Zach's face, tracing the line of stubble with his fingers. "Was it okay?"

Zach laughed through trembling breaths. "I came so hard I think I might have broken something, and you don't know if it was okay?"

Leith wiped a tear from the corner of Zach's eye. "But...you're crying."

Zach shook his head. "Side effect of great sex. I'm not crying. I'm too happy to cry."

"No tears of joy from you?" Leith asked, his own cock still hard and aching.

Zach seemed to notice, and kissed Leith's lips. "Only on the day I knew you'd live…and in the rose garden when you kissed me. When I knew you loved me still."

He bent to take Leith into his mouth, and Leith blinked back his own tears.

𝕣 𝕣 𝕣

The next two days were amazing. Leith couldn't think of another word to describe them. They made love, and swam in the lake, and Leith hiked into the mountains while Zach straggled thirty yards behind and complained loudly that he preferred other ways to get sweaty.

Leith found Zach strangely easy to talk to, and he laughed more than he could remember laughing in his entire life. Nearly everything about Zach made him *feel* things—happiness, amusement, and butterflies in his stomach.

Just listening to Zach talk about something simple like his favorite movies—all old Hollywood westerns starring John Wayne—made his heart clench with a silly delirious feeling that left him on the verge of giggling like a kid. And little things like the way Zach danced to pop songs as he cooked, so silly and without shame, made Leith want to kiss him until they fell on the floor and ended up having sex again.

Or the way Zach made him feel safe enough to talk about things he didn't tell anyone else. Like how he'd lost his virginity to Jennifer Dunaway at a party when he was sixteen after being in love with her from afar for over a year.

He'd thought they were going to be together afterward, and he'd been so in love that night, thinking she finally understood why they were meant to be. But the next morning she wanted nothing to do with him, and ended up going out with a violinist with glasses and a weird haircut.

"Who was your first?" Leith asked. He was sitting on the ground beside Zach, poking at the campfire they'd made,

139

shirtless because it was really too hot for a fire. The sky was clear and full of stars, and he'd pointed some out to Zach earlier.

"I don't remember his name," Zach said, staring into the flames. He yawned.

"What?" Leith couldn't imagine not remembering the name of someone he'd had sex with. The last three years being an entirely valid exception, of course.

Zach shrugged. "I was thirteen. I was at this really cool party with some older kids, and I didn't really know him."

Leith took a moment to process this.

Zach waved his hand as though pushing the subject away. "It was completely consensual, and I had a very good time. The main thing is, it set me on the path to a very enjoyable period of extreme sexual promiscuity. This was good, because eventually that path of bold derring-do led me to taking a job on a cruise ship. I traveled the world, fulfilling my every lust for life and strange men."

"Oh." Leith didn't know what to think.

Zach smiled, poking at the fire. "And *that* was good because when the time came for me to settle down in New York—which isn't necessarily my absolute favorite city in the world, but it's the place where I found *you*—I had no wild oats left to sow, and no regrets about committing to someone I cared about so much. The way I see, not knowing my first's name seems relatively unimportant in the scheme of it all, because everything about my life led me here to this moment with you."

Leith nodded slowly, his lower lip out a bit as he tried to appear as though he understood where Zach was coming from. But casual sex had always seemed so unappealing to him that he truly didn't get it. He knew he was an oddity in that regard.

Unless...something had changed with him. Maybe he and Zach were into threesomes, or group sex. What did he know? Leith shuddered, and felt sick at the idea of sharing Zach with anyone else. "Do we...?" Leith asked, his nose wrinkling with disgust.

Zach looked confused. "Do we...what?"

"You know—with other people?"

Zach's eyebrows almost disappeared into his hairline. "No, Leith. Don't you know yourself better than that?"

Leith sighed with relief. "Well, I do, but then again I didn't know I was gay, or bi, or whatever I am until I met you."

"Yes," Zach said, teasing. "I remember."

Leith smirked. "I wonder what other things I don't know about myself. I mean, that's a big thing to sneak up on someone."

"A lot of guys don't realize until they're older. Especially guys who like girls too. I think you always thought that the attraction you felt for women was as good as it got. Until you met me." He lifted his chin proudly. "Then you realized that maybe you'd just been on the wrong train the whole time."

Leith considered this. "Was I ever with another man? Or just you?"

"Just me. But I really don't think if something happened between us you'd go back to women. I think you'd date men."

Leith frowned, searching his heart to see if he agreed, but he didn't know. He just knew that Zach and everything about him was what he wanted. He wondered if he'd ever agreed with Zach on that point before. Maybe there had been other men he'd been attracted to, but now he just didn't remember.

"In prison..." Leith trailed off.

"Yeah?" Zach prodded.

"Well, there were guys that I'd watch working out in the gym. I'd notice their muscles and how their bare arms looked when they were slick with sweat. It was never the guys who were really muscular, though. It was usually the smaller guys.

141

The prettier ones."

Zach laughed a little. "And you told me once about Sweets Swinson. Look where that got you."

Hell, that's where.

Leith's memories of the last illegal fight were vivid. He could still smell the sweat of the men, hear the roar of their voices, and feel that final crunch under his fist as he'd taken the kid down for the win.

He also remembered Sweets, though it wasn't with the same heart-pounding excitement he felt when he was nineteen. No, now it was a little bit of nausea and a whole lot of anger.

"I was an idiot," Leith said. "I never should have taken up with Sweets."

"The dick wants what the dick wants," Zach said.

Leith huffed. He didn't find it funny. He didn't even know if he'd really wanted Sweets that way or if it had been some other kind of sick chemistry between them that had led to Leith always wanting to please the man.

"I remember when I met him," Leith said. But he didn't remember when he met Zach. How strange. Unless he counted the day Zach had walked into his hospital room. But Sweets, hell yeah, he remembered meeting Sweets. "I'd been in a fight at school trying to pick up some extra cash to help my dad out. He was gambling again."

Zach poked at the fire with a stick and cocked his head, listening to Leith with his eyebrows low and sympathetic.

"My dad was always gambling. He'd go straight for a while but then just as soon as it looked like we'd finally get our ass out of whatever financial crack he'd gotten us into, he'd go right back to it. Like me with fighting, I guess."

"There are some similarities," Zach agreed, his voice quiet.

"Dad was in a mess again when I met Sweets. And Arthur

wouldn't help out. Joseph's Teeth was finally up and running, bringing in good cash. He'd even offered for me to come live with him in the city and work there, but he'd said the offer was only good if I promised not to give a dime to Dad." Leith snorted. "How could I do that? He was my dad."

Was. It looked like he was getting better at accepting that his dad was really gone.

"He didn't want your dad to take him and his business down through you, I guess."

"Right. I mean, I understand it. I do. But back then I didn't. Okay, the truth is I guess maybe I still don't."

"I know."

"But Sweets wasn't like that. He was confident and told me he could help me help my dad, which was pretty much exactly what I wanted to hear. The fact that he was charismatic and— yeah, pretty I guess—helped. I wanted to impress him, and he found my fighting damn impressive."

"MMA stuff, right? Not boxing like now."

"Right. I always liked good, old-fashioned boxing best, but when Sweets came along he convinced me to use my other fighting skills. It was so easy at first. Underground fights where I'd make a ton of cash. More than I needed—more than Dad needed."

"But then Sweets got greedy," Zach said, poking at the fire some more.

"You know this story."

"Tell me again. I want you to remember telling me. It's important."

Leith cleared his throat and tilted his head back to look into the sky, the stars obscured by the light of their fire. "I got greedy too. Sweets told me about a fight in Florida, an illegal round of backyard cage fights. It was four times my usual take."

"You made it through four bouts."

"Right. The fifth was when it all went to shit. Everyone was supposed to be at least eighteen, which was pointless in its own way since what we were doing was illegal in Florida period. The fact that my opponent wasn't actually eighteen ended up being a big deal to me, though, didn't it?"

"You didn't know. You trusted them."

He could still taste the sweat. Hear the cheers, and smell the stench of cheap beer. "I won. But then he started puking blood. It was unreal. Everyone panicked—they just broke and ran. Sweets tried to convince me to leave, too, but I couldn't just let that kid...I mean, he was...there was blood everywhere and it just didn't stop."

"So you called 911."

"I did."

"And you waited for them so he wouldn't be alone."

Leith could smell the copper of blood as he whispered, "Yeah."

"And he lived because of you."

"He also almost died because of me."

"Well, you got to spend two years in prison for that, so I figure you paid plenty for that lack of judgment. Time to stop flogging that dead horse. He lived. You did your time for your bad choices. It's done. And now you're here with me. Life led you right into my arms."

Leith snorted. "You're kind of a hippie romantic."

"You're kind of determined to beat yourself up about stuff you can't control. And you're a romantic, too, so we're matched there."

"You make me feel good," he blurted. "Really good."

Zach crawled over, pushing him down on the ground and climbing on top of him, running his hands over Leith's chest. "I can't help it. I just know exactly what you need."

"Oh really?"

"Oh yes."

Leith kissed him, and thought that Zach did know what he needed. But he also sensed that in some way he didn't yet understand, Leith held the cards between them. Somehow that made him want to protect Zach, and that feeling always made him want to fuck him.

A few minutes later Zach was riding him, his head thrown back and his skin beautiful with red, orange, and blue flickers from the campfire. Leith gripped Zach's hips and watched his cock bounce, the strings of pre-come glistening in the flame's glow.

🎀 🎀 🎀

Packing up the car on the last morning, Zach came over to Leith and wrapped his arms around his waist, hugging him tight. "I don't want to leave. I want to stay here with you forever."

Leith sighed and hugged Zach close, his eyes drawn again to the mountains and the trees, marking them in his memory. He wanted to stay, too, but he knew they couldn't. It was time. He had to face his new-old life, and figure out what to do with his future. But he understood. If he could, he'd stop time and stay in this place with Zach forever.

"Zach?" Leith whispered. "No matter what happens, I'll never forget this time here with you."

"Is that a promise?"

"It's a promise," Leith said, hugging Zach even closer. He could give his word without reservation. As far as he knew, he'd never been so in love before.

LATER THAT DAY
VLOG ENTRY #8

INT. GAS STATION BATHROOM
Zach's face is big on the screen, and he talks quietly as he holds up his phone.

ZACH
My loves, I don't have much time. Leith is filling up the car, but I wanted to tell you—things are good here. He's different, it's true, but I'm so in love with him that I'm surprised I haven't floated away on a cloud.

I think it's the grief that grounds me. It's hard to explain how I feel—how mixed up I get sometimes. But I hold it together for him. I have to, because he can't know that I miss anything. I only want him to feel my love for him.

Do you remember how I asked if it could hurt more if he died? The answer is yes. To have him here with me? It's worth all the rest of it: the pain of losing him, and how much I miss our old life. It's worth it.

It's confusing, I know. I live with it every day. I'm happy, and I love him, and I miss him every second of every day. Crazy isn't it?

I'd better go. I'll introduce you another day. I just wanted to record this moment before we go back to the real world. For now, just know that I'm happy.

Chapter Nine

The apartment was clean and neat, and utterly unfamiliar to him. There were a ton of people there—faces he recognized from the hospital, like Marian and Ava, but there were others he didn't know at all. Arthur's girlfriend, Miyoko, was a pretty brunette who was very well dressed. She was indeed on the young side, but Arthur had hearts in his eyes when he looked at her, and Leith liked seeing him happy.

Leith noticed that Zach seemed to act a bit big brotherly toward her, and it made him want to kiss Zach. He thought it might be an odd reaction, but there was very little about Zach that didn't result in Leith wanting to kiss him.

A girl named Vanessa said she had worked with Leith at Blue Flight before his injury. Ava's brother, David—at least Leith thought that was his name—also said he worked at the bar. Leith noticed that David stood by the window eating chips and staring at Zach's cousin, Janelle, an auburn haired waif who was very beautiful. But he remembered Zach saying that he didn't like her, and he waited almost eagerly to see what he'd think of her now. It was like gossip about someone else's life, only kind of interesting because it applied to *him*.

There were a few other people around whose names Leith didn't catch, and he didn't really want to ask again. At some point Arthur sidled over to put his arm around Zach's sister, Maddie—a brunette who looked like a shorter, thinner version of Zach—and the interaction seemed a bit tense for some reason.

"What's up with that?" he asked, nodding toward them.

"They're friends now, but there was a time when Maddie thought there might have been more. There were hurt feelings all around."

Leith wasn't surprised by this given his brother's romantic shenanigans, but he just gave a closed-mouth smile and said nothing. Everyone seemed to be having a good time, so despite the fact that he was already tired and growing weary of the strangers, Leith let the party go on.

Arthur and Miyoko danced to a slow song, and Maddie danced with Zach, smiling and laughing with him. Leith didn't want to dance with anyone other than Zach, so he made his escape.

"The bathroom?" Leith asked Marian after the third glass of celebratory sparkling water. The telling glances around the room let him know that everyone had forgotten he wasn't who he used to be—that he didn't know where the bathroom was, or the silverware, or the towels, or his bedroom.

"This way," Zach said, breaking away from Maddie and pointing toward a door halfway down the hallway.

"You don't need to escort me," Leith said, smiling. "I think I can find it now."

Zach let him go, his brow creasing, and Leith paused in the doorway to mouth the word, "*Relax.*"

Zach smiled and nodded, turning back to his sister, and Leith found the bathroom without any trouble.

It was decorated in turquoise and white, with a clamshell-shaped rug in front of the sink. He turned the faucet on and off, feeling the cool porcelain of the handles on his palms. He sighed. Nothing. He didn't remember the bathroom at all. He wondered who'd picked out the beach scene shower curtain. He tilted his head and pondered it, trying to decide if he even liked it. Had he ever?

It was quiet, and though he could hear the chatter and clinking of silverware on plates seeping under the door, he felt safer in the bathroom, alone and unobserved. Everyone seemed great; really nice, and happy to see him. All in all he thought he must have built a pretty nice life for himself before the boxing match that took it all away.

Leith sighed. Boxing, that was something he hadn't let himself think about yet. There was a time when he couldn't live without it, but now he didn't have a choice. What would he do with his life now? Could he make himself believe that what he really wanted to do was become a physical education teacher?

He sat down in the bathtub, his feet hanging over the edge.

There was a knock at the door, and Zach's said, "Leith?"

"Come in," Leith called, leaning his head back against the tile wall.

"Hey." Zach shut the door behind him, his eyes worried. "Are you getting tired?"

Leith shrugged a little and patted the space next to him in the tub. Zach smiled and climbed in, his tennis shoes hanging next to Leith's and his thigh pressed against Leith's leg.

"How do you feel?" Zach asked.

"Like I've been dropped into the middle of a conversation. I just keep nodding along like I know what's going on."

Zach sighed and rested his head on Leith's shoulder. "I'm sorry. I should have told them all to stay away. They just wanted to see you so much."

"No, it's okay. I'd want to see me too."

Zach chuckled, but then grew serious again and pressed a kiss to Leith's neck. "They need to understand that we're starting over again. From scratch. Everything."

Leith kissed Zach's forehead and said nothing, because he wasn't sure he agreed. Zach seemed bent on moving them forward, going on ahead and ignoring the past, but Leith didn't know how much longer he could do that. There were things he wanted to know—not just because he felt he deserved it, but because he thought they might help him plan for the future.

"I've been thinking about boxing," Leith said.

Zach took hold of Leith's hand. "I thought you might. But remember what the doctors said?"

Leith shrugged. The doctors didn't want him boxing again. Period. They said the risk was too great. He already suffered from a traumatic brain injury, and he should thank his lucky stars that three years was all he'd lost. "Did I ever tell you about how I got started in it? I probably did."

Zach smiled faintly. "Tell me again."

Leith took a slow breath, remembering the first boxing lesson his father had given him. He'd been ten, and his mother had fretted that the gloves were too heavy for his hands. But his father had slapped the back of his head affectionately and said, "Head down!" before throwing a punch and then demonstrating how Leith should block it with his gloves.

"Dad started out teaching me and Arthur, but later we got a real coach. I remember Dad splurged—and given all the trouble he had with money, it was really a big splurge—to send us to the local boxing club to train with Matt Nash."

"A local champion from your dad's generation," Zach murmured, leaning his head against Leith's shoulder.

"I miss that old boxing club. I miss Matt." He sighed. "Those were the good days before mom died and everything went to hell."

"I know."

"But that's not it. I miss the ritual of it: taping my hands and putting on the gloves. I miss the feeling of my fist connecting. I miss the smell of sweat. I miss the sounds. It's so pure for me."

"It's joy."

"Yeah."

Leith smiled, warmth and rightness flooding him that Zach

knew him so well that he could fill in the blanks for him. Leith kissed Zach's hand. "If I started up again, I don't know how good I'd be. My doctors say that my speed and coordination was affected by the trauma to my brain. I might be able to get it back, though. If I trained very hard."

Zach was silent and still. When he spoke his voice was strained. "I nearly lost you. When I think of you in the ring, I think of the ambulance, and the days I sat there thinking you were going to die. I remember when they told me your memory of me was gone, and I remember seeing you that day, and knowing that you didn't know me, and how I—" Zach broke off. "I admit it. I don't want you to box or fight at all, and if begging would stop you from doing it, I would."

Leith squeezed Zach's hand. Part of him felt he should be more annoyed, angry even, or that he should put up a fight. But he was too tired to summon the energy, and he wasn't sure he wanted to be angry anyway.

❀ ❀ ❀

Leith stood beside his bed, looking around the room. There were photos on the wall of him with apparent friends he didn't recognize, a punching bag hanging in the corner, and various items that clearly held some sort of meaning for whoever he used to be. He had no clue what they meant or who they were from.

"Well," Zach said, seeming suddenly shy. "I'll leave you. There's clean-up to do, and Janelle hasn't—"

"Zach, wait." Leith looked around the room. "Where do you sleep? In here with me, right?"

Zach's hands fluttered nervously. "Well, we used to—but you probably want your space until you're more comfortable. I moved my things back to my old room when they were going to discharge you the first time, before—well, before, and—"

"Zach, why would I want you to sleep in another room?"

He looked small with his arms crossed protectively over his chest, and his face dangerously vulnerable. Leith wanted to shut the door and do something about that look.

"In the hospital, for a while I thought about just going somewhere else. I came back here because of you, Zach. Because of how I feel when I'm with you." Leith took him in his arms and kicked the door shut behind him. "Understand?"

Zach nodded, and Leith held him close for a few minutes, breathing in the comforting scent of his cologne before starting at the buttons on his shirt. It had been since the prior night by the campfire, and Leith couldn't believe how long ago that seemed. He was already hard, and had been since Zach's face had gone all sweet and defenseless. He didn't waste any time getting Zach onto the bed.

Before long Zach was on his hands and knees, gripping the bed sheets and burying his noises in the pillow. Leith groaned at the sight, biting his lower lip and slamming into Zach harder just to see him squirm again. Yes, the apartment and room were unfamiliar, and the party had been confusing and stressful, but sharing *this* with Zach washed all of that away in a rush of pleasure and need. He ran his hands over the clenching muscles in Zach's back before grabbing Zach's shoulders and fucking him hard.

"Yes," Zach cried out, reaching back to stroke a hand down Leith's leg.

"Do you like it hard like this?"

"Oh fuck, yes. Harder even."

Leith kissed his neck, licking along his ear and pounding his ass in quick strong thrusts. Nothing but Zach existed as he raced to the edge of orgasm, and he threw his head back, searching for it, craving it to blot out the uncomfortable night and the looming anxiety about his future.

A noise caught his attention, and he swung his head toward the suddenly open door and the person standing there.

Leith pulled out of Zach, who flipped over, looking bewildered. Leith quickly jerked the sheets up to cover him and rolled out of bed and into a fighting stance before he even fully registered who had intruded into their space.

"What the fuck?" he shouted.

Zach's cousin Janelle smirked. "Huh. I always figured Zach would be on top, what with the way you always let him boss you around."

Pulse pounding and seeing red, Leith roared, "Get the fuck out before I throw you out!" He felt Zach's hand on his trembling back.

"Leith, calm down."

"Jeez, chill out, fighter. And use the lock next time!"

Leith clenched his fists, determined to master himself, and repeated the mantra Arthur had drilled into him when he was just a kid: it's never okay to punch a girl.

Janelle wriggled her fingers in a cutesy wave and took her time closing the door.

"Come on," Zach said, tugging on Leith's arm until he joined him again on the bed. "She's gone now."

"I think I want to murder her," Leith muttered, still struggling to get his temper in check.

Groaning, Zach flopped back on the bed and buried his face in the pillow. "No, you won't get the pleasure. I'm going to murder her first." He looked up at Leith, his hair mussed and chest still flushed with arousal. "I told you that you didn't like her."

"I should have believed you," Leith said. "God, I was really damn close too."

"Yeah? You were?"

"So fucking close."

Zach looked up, his lips in a pout and his eyes pleading. "Leith...can you still...?"

Leith closed his eyes and took a few calming breaths. He opened them again and nodded. The relief in Zach's eyes warmed him, and he laughed. "Did you get left a little needy?"

Zach bit his lip. "Desperate. You got me all crazy. Please, Leith..." He got back on his hands and knees.

Leith pushed Zach's legs apart and climbed between them. As he checked the condom and shoved in, he remembered what Janelle had said. He settled his cock deep in Zach's ass and bent to whisper, "Do you ever do this to me?"

Zach twisted around for a wet kiss. "My God, yes. You love it."

Leith shuddered and started rocking, grabbing Zach's hips and holding them still when Zach squirmed against the sheets. "Let's do that soon," he whispered. Zach made a desperate noise and grabbed his own cock, jerking it hard and fast while Leith fucked him.

❀ ❀ ❀

Dr. Thakur sat beside Leith on the bench near the roses. "How's outside life treating you?"

Leith ran his hands over his jeans and tilted his head back to the sky. "Sure beats a prison," he said, and then cracked a smile. "It's good. Things are...good."

"How are you spending your days?"

Leith shrugged. He wasn't doing a lot right now, just trying to sort things out. Zach let him behind the counter when things got busy at Blue Flight, but for the most part, Leith looked at his books from CUNY, and thought about his future. He didn't know if he felt passionate about a career in physical education anymore. When he tried to write down a list of pros and cons, he hid the paper from Zach, not wanting him to see his handwriting. "Trying to figure out my future."

"The future is like a thousand suns," Dr. Thakur said, stretching his legs out and crossing his ankles.

"Really bright?" Leith asked, chuckling.

"Yes," Dr. Thakur said, and then shook his head. "You think I'm full of bullshit, don't you, Leith?"

"No, of course not." Leith hoped he sounded convincing.

"And how is Zachariah?"

"He's…great," Leith said, smiling as he remembered Zach bustling around Blue Flight earlier, alternately telling Vanessa where to put the vodka and instructing Leith on which buses to take to get to the clinic for his appointment. Zach was so cute when he was being bossy.

"Hmm. No problems with feeling overwhelmed? Somehow I don't believe that."

Leith smirked. "I'm fine. When I feel stressed I go running or punch the bag in my room for a while."

"Those are both pro-active ways to deal with your frustration."

Leith shrugged his agreement.

"What has been the hardest thing so far?"

Where to start? Maybe when Zach had shown him around the bathroom before bed that first night. *"This is your toothbrush and our toothpaste—Marian keeps hers here, but we don't use it unless we run out before we can buy more. Here's Ava's; we never use hers because it tastes disgusting, and having dirty teeth is better. This is where we keep the towels, and the spare toilet paper goes here. This is your shampoo, that's Ava's…"* and on and on. Leith had felt like he should be taking notes, or that he was eight and being guided around a friend's house before a sleepover.

"But you've settled in since then?" Dr. Thakur asked.

"Yeah. I've had weird things happen, though."

"Like what?"

"Well, like one day I was at my brother and Zach's bar, and I realized I knew how to mix drinks. Even drinks I don't remember from before."

"How did that feel?"

"Good. Right. But then…"

"What happened?"

"Zach just looked so *hopeful,* and I realized he wants me to get my memories back."

"Does he?"

Leith sighed. "I don't know."

"What does he say?"

"He says he wants to move on."

"I see. And do you want to move on?"

"Maybe. I don't know."

Dr. Thakur nodded. "And the anger?"

"I feel calm when I'm with Zach, but yeah, sometimes I still get angry." He remembered Janelle walking in on them making love. "But it's not too much. I can control it."

He sighed, remembering the day he'd volunteered to get something out of the storage room for Zach and put in the combination to the door without even thinking.

He slammed his fist against the storage room wall. "Leith!" Zach cried. He'd put his arms around Leith's waist from behind and rubbed his stomach soothingly. "Please, don't get so worked up."

Leith shook free and paced the storage room, realizing he knew where the lemons were kept—in the back corner—and not wanting to tell Zach that he knew.

"What are you thinking of?" Dr. Thakur asked him.

"A day I got angry."

"With Zach?"

He shook his head. "With myself."

"Why?"

"Because...I can't remember."

Leith hadn't been able to take the look in Zach's eyes that day in the storage room, not when he knew Zach *wanted* him to remember. And if Zach wanted him to remember, that meant Zach wanted the old him back, even now.

"You can't remember why you got angry?"

"No," Leith huffed. "I'm angry because I can't remember." He brought his hands up to his mouth, fingers steepled, and took deep breaths, feeling as though he were shaking down to his core.

"Leith?" Dr. Thakur asked.

But in his mind it was Zach's voice he heard.

"Leith, talk to me. Please."

"Dr. Thakur says I should swim against the current. Not let myself get washed away in it."

Zach had nodded and pressed his cheek to Leith's shoulder. "I won't let you get washed away."

"I only remember pointless things. Combination locks. How to mix drinks. But I don't remember what's important to you."

"Hey, hey," Zach said, moving in front of Leith and cupping his face in his hands. "You know who we are to each other, and that's all I need. Everything else is past. It's gone, and all that's left is us. We don't need anything else."

Leith swallowed thickly. "What if I do?"

Zach shook his head. "You don't have to know anything other than this," and he kissed Leith's lips so softly and sweetly that Leith's knees buckled a little. "Can you tell me more about this memory you're caught up in?"

Leith shrugged and tried to put it into words. He felt a little nauseous, but it helped to get it out. "Zach hasn't accepted it, I don't think."

"What?"

"That I'm never going to remember our past. He doesn't want to talk about it because he hasn't dealt with the fact that this is all we have. This time together now."

"That last part is very true, but I can't speak to Zach's state of mind. He's been a closed door to me from almost the beginning. He doesn't talk about the times before?"

"Almost never. Only when I ask, and then only to answer my questions. Sometimes he'll even try to avoid that by telling me all we need is each other here and now. On the surface it sounds like he's accepted the truth, but underneath, I don't think he has."

"That's very astute. If it causes him pain to remember, do you feel entitled to make him talk about it?"

"Not really. But the old Leith deserves to be remembered, doesn't he?"

"Everyone deserves to be remembered."

"And Zach's the one who remembers him. I just wish it didn't hurt him so much that the old Leith is gone. It makes me feel like I'm not good enough."

"But you are good enough, Leith. Just the way you are."

"Gee, thanks, doc. I feel all better now."

Dr. Thakur snorted. "I've mentioned my wife is from India. Her grandmother taught her many things, and she walks around our house spouting wisdom left and right. Occasionally I'm reminded of the warning about throwing pearls before swine, so I sometimes attempt to be less of a pig and listen to her."

Leith raised his eyebrows and wondered where this was going. "Uh-huh."

"Last night she said to me, 'Krishna told us that he was the taste of pure water, the sound of every voice and noise, the radiance of the sun and moon, and the courage of human beings.' And I, in my own infinite wisdom, thought to myself, 'Now that's what I'll tell Leith tomorrow, so that he can feel that he's getting something meaningful from our discussion.'"

Leith was bewildered. "Okay," he replied, nodding.

"Krishna, by the way, represents the vastness of everything, and that includes the future. He's bigger and brighter than a thousand suns. Do you understand? Larger than any future—mine, yours, everyone's. He's big enough to encompass the past *and* the future, *and* every conceivable moment of both."

"Dr. Thakur, is this religious instruction, or am I here for psychiatric counseling?"

"Some would say there's very little difference between the two, but let me ask you a few questions, and perhaps we'll come back around to what I was just telling you."

"Sure."

"Have you been thinking about that little bird lately?"

"The kinglet?"

"Yes, the one you thought of fairly often in the beginning. The one you wanted to help."

Leith hadn't thought about the kinglet in a while now, finding his focus was entirely on Zach. "No."

"Boxing?"

Leith cleared his throat and looked down at his hands. He shrugged and squinted up into the sunny sky. "I don't know."

Dr. Thakur was silent for several minutes, and Leith listened to the birds rustling in the bushes.

Finally, Dr. Thakur said, "Human courage is a divine thing, you realize. It is right up there with the radiance of the moon, and the taste of pure water, and the light of a thousand suns. You, Leith, are incredibly courageous. I've watched you come to grips with a very difficult situation and face the loss of your father, your memory, and your idea of who your mother had been. I've seen you embrace desire for another man despite your confusion, and plunge into a life of strangers who love you. None are easy feats."

"Poetry didn't pay enough as a career?" Leith asked.

"No, annoying my patients suffering from amnesia pays much more."

Leith smiled. "Yeah, yeah, go on."

"How about I stop talking now? Why don't you talk some more?"

"About what?"

"I don't know. Why don't you tell me what you think about courage," Dr. Thakur said.

"Courage," Leith repeated aloud, studying his fingers. After a few minutes of silence, he said, "Everyone says boxing isn't a smart thing to do. My neurologists advise against it. Zach says it frightens him."

"Fear is a strong motivator."

Leith thought about the future—the long stretch of it ahead of him, endless. It would roll on and on without him even after he was dead. He only had so much of it for himself. "Those memories, they were only three years. I've got an entire future waiting," Leith said softly. "I don't want to waste it being afraid."

"Exactly," Dr. Thakur agreed.

"Dr. Thakur, are you telling me to box again?"

"Of course not. I'm talking about Krishna, and my wife, and courage, and thousands of suns, and all kinds of madness. You're the one talking about boxing."

INT. BLUE FLIGHT – BOOTH
Zach sits alone in a booth in the empty restaurant. He salutes the camera.

ZACH

I'm in a bit of a mood tonight, my loves. Rumor has it that Leith is considering boxing again. And the person spreading this information is Leith himself, so I'm pretty sure it's true.

He sighs.

I'm trying to be supportive because I know what the sport means to him, but I can't cheer him on. It's funny. I remember the old days when I'd watch him train. The way my heart would burst with pride and—yes, something a lot dirtier than pride—whenever I watched him in the ring. All that muscle, and sweat, and the power. God, that *power*.

But now when I think of boxing, I just remember the smell of that ever-present antiseptic in ICU, and I hear the beeps of those damn machines and...

Fuck him!

I just got him back and now I'm going to lose him again.

He rubs his eyes.

Fuck, I feel so guilty even saying this out loud, which is why I'm saying it to you and not to Marian or Ava...and definitely not to Leith. I could never look him in the face and say these words to him, because they're so ungrateful and awful. I mean, I know, from the bottom of my heart and soul, I truly know how lucky I am to still have him in my life. But, my loves? I think I'm a bad person. Because here's the thing—*I miss him so much.*

I know, I know. Technically he's here with me. He's alive and he's so much the same, but he's *so* different too. He's not the same man he was before. He's like a colt finding his legs. My Leith, my sweet Leith, was cocky and sure of himself, and when I wavered or got scared, when I started to flake on my life or on us, he'd plow on through. Like *of course* everything was fine, and *of course* I could manage whatever was happening.

Now I'm supporting him, and I miss his bullshit bravado so damn much. I need someone to just bully me into believing we're going to be fine. That I can do this, and that we're okay. But I can't have that. Because that person was Leith.

Some days I feel like he died after all.

He covers his face.

I'm so ashamed to say that. So fucking ashamed.

He drops his hands and clears his throat.

No, ignore that. Ignore all that whiny, needy crap and...don't. Just please tell me everything's going to be okay? I need to hear that so much right now. Please. Tell me he won't box, or that if he does, he's going to be safe, and tell me it's okay to miss him, because I need someone to say that to me. Please...just, God, I wish he could hold me right now.

He wipes hastily at his face.

I hear him. I should go.

LEITH (*off screen*)
Are you coming up to bed?

Zach clears his throat and smiles.

ZACH
Yep! Just give me a second, okay?

LEITH (*off screen*)
Anything you want.

ZACH
Whispers to the camera.

Oh, how I wish he could deliver on that.

Talk to you all later.

Chapter Ten

"Are you going to take me? I've been out of the hospital over a month and I'm going whether you want me to or not."

Arthur sighed. "Okay, I guess I can show you around. Just don't tell Zach I took you."

"I can handle it, Arthur," Leith said, glaring at his brother. "I think it's about time that I handled some things for myself."

When he walked into the boxing club he was greeted by grunts of exertion and the slap and whap of gloves on skin and bags. He took a deep breath, the scents of sweat and mildew from the showers filling his nose.

"This is great," he murmured, and then stopped in his tracks as the room grew quiet and all eyes turned to him. Every face showed a mix of concern and gladness, expressions that Leith was sick of seeing. It hadn't even occurred to him that the men here would know him, but of course they would. He'd nearly been their champion.

"Leith!" A man with blond hair and expressive blue eyes approached, glancing over his shoulder as some guys fell in behind him. "Hey, bud. How are you?"

Leith hadn't had to deal with this yet. Almost everyone he'd seen since leaving the hospital already knew about his injury.

"We were all worried about you," the man went on. "Most of us testified as witnesses, even though they had it on video."

Leith nodded and plastered a friendly smile on his face. "I'm sorry, but the injury damaged my memory. I'm afraid I don't remember you." He paused and looked around at everyone gathering. "Or any of you. Sorry."

The glances exchanged around the room were full of meaning both obvious, such as pity, and less obvious. Leith cleared this throat. "I wanted to have a look at the club. I was thinking of training again."

"I'm Marvin," the man said, sticking out his hand. "I'll show you around."

"Jerry," another guy said, and Leith shook his hand too.

The men filed around him, shaking hands if they had their gloves off, or gently punching him on the shoulder if they didn't. Marvin walked him around, explaining the club dues and indicating the showers and the water cooler.

Leith stopped by the bulletin board next to the changing room. There was a news article tacked up, and his heart skipped a beat as he peered at the photo. It was him in the practice ring. His boxing gloves framed Zach's face, and he was kissing him. His eyes were drawn to the headline: *Can Brooklyn's Gay Boxer Beat the Odds?*

"Zach," Leith said, touching the photo and smiling a little. They looked so happy, and his heart ached at the expression of joy and pride on Zach's face. He wanted to see that expression directed at *him*, not at the old version of him smiling in the photo. He gritted his teeth a little, working to gain control over the jealousy he felt.

"We put that up after you got hurt. We...all of us...wanted to remember better times for you," Marvin said, standing with his hands on his hips. He shook his head. "That was a real surprise to some of us at first, you know. You and another guy. But you were so defiant about it and obviously in love. I was impressed with you even then. You're still together?"

Leith nodded, staring at the photo until all he saw were black and white dots, pixels swimming in his eyes.

"He's a good guy. He came by after the accident once to get your stuff. He was really torn up." Marvin sighed, nodding at

165

the photo. "I'm still sorry about what happened after that article came out."

Leith stared at him, the hair on his arms standing up. "What happened after?"

Marvin blinked. "You don't know?"

"Know what?"

"You should ask your boyfriend," Marvin said, his face creasing as he backed away. "Listen, I need to get back to training. But we'd love to have you back. See you later?"

"Yeah, sure," Leith said, turning back to the newspaper article and photo. The smiles in the photo were so pure. Would Zach ever look at *him* like that?

He knew there was no answer—at least not yet. But what had happened when the article was published? His stomach clenched thinking of the possibilities. Leith took the article down and folded it carefully into his pocket. At least that was one question he could get to the bottom of.

🎀 🎀 🎀

Marian sat forward on her chair at the dining table and looked at the newspaper article with a tender expression. "I always loved how you would just kiss him there in front of everyone. It was so romantic." She sighed. "It was so *sweet.*"

"What happened, though?" Leith asked, not wanting to hear about the wonderful former Leith who had said romantic things to his boyfriend and kissed him in the boxing ring. His need to know about himself battled with his frustration and jealousy in ways he couldn't understand. "Something bad happened because of that article, didn't it?"

"Oh. That," Marian said, frowning. "You'd better talk to Zach about it."

Leith took the article and studied the photo again. "He doesn't talk about before my injury. He says he wants to move on." Leith admitted, "I think it hurts him to remember."

"Well, yeah. Of course it does. He was devastated; absolutely torn to pieces afterward. He was like a zombie. I'd never seen him cry until then. And when you didn't remember him? He was inconsolable. I've never seen anything like it." Marian paused. "Really, you should talk to Zach."

Leith sighed and dropped the article on the table between them. "I can't. It hurts him and I don't want to do that."

Marian nodded. "I understand. He's been through a lot." She touched the newspaper clipping with her fingertip. "You really want to know?"

"Yes," Leith said. "It's my *life*, Marian."

"Okay. After you came out, there were some pretty big problems. Some guys at the boxing club weren't too keen on having a queer working out there. You weren't going to be frightened away, so a few of them—one was your friend Marvin's younger brother—decided the best way to scare you off was to get at you through Zach."

"They harassed him?"

"More than that. They waited in the alley outside Blue Flight one night for Zach to bring the trash out. He used to insist on doing it himself. At the time he was trying to quit smoking. He'd gotten down to one a day, and he'd save it as a reward and smoke it out by the garbage dumpsters."

"He smoked?"

"Yeah. You hated it."

"Is that why he quit?"

"One of the reasons I'm sure, but anyway, it was part of his plan to quit. If he was only allowed to smoke one and it had to be out in the alley by the dumpster, he figured it'd be easier to make the final break. I think you know where I'm going with this story, Leith."

"They hurt him?"

"They did, but the cops broke it up fast. Miyoko called them when she heard the commotion, and luckily there was a squad car just around the corner. Even luckier, you'd taught Zach how to defend himself, though he was really outnumbered."

"How bad was it?"

"Cracked ribs, black eye, and busted lip. It wasn't too bad."

Squeezing his hands into fists, Leith trembled. "Not too bad? Jesus."

"You were pretty scary. I was glad they arrested the guys because if they'd been free? Who knows what might've happened."

"Did they go to jail?"

"Community service and kicked out of the boxing club. Fucking courts. Fucking world."

Leith's jaw creaked as he clenched down.

"Don't even think about it, buddy. It was a long time ago now and Zach isn't interested in revenge."

"Yeah, sure. I know. Thank you." He imagined how good it would feel for his fist to connect with the attackers' flesh and crunch their bones.

Keys jangled and the front door opened. "Hello?" Zach called.

Marian squeezed Leith's arm and grabbed her purse. "I was just heading out." She breezed by Zach and closed the door behind her.

Zach hovered in the little front hallway. "Did I interrupt something?"

It had taken only a few minutes to relate the story, but Leith now couldn't imagine not knowing it. Somehow it made Zach more precious to him, and he wanted to touch him and kiss him, to wipe away the forgotten past held in Marian's words. But he hesitated. He had a feeling Zach wouldn't be glad Leith knew this particular truth—or how he'd discovered it.

He took a deep breath. "I went to the boxing club today."

Zach said nothing for a moment, but his mouth tightened as he pressed his lips together. "Oh? So you're definitely going to box again?"

"I think so."

Zach's jaw clenched and he strode to the kitchen, grabbed a cloth, and began to wipe the counter with quick strokes. "It's your choice, but your brain is already injured, and another incident could lead to you being nothing but mush," Zach gritted out, his face flushed.

"Zach..." Leith went to stand by the fridge. "I understand how you're feeling."

Zach blew out some air and said nothing, continuing to scrub invisible stains.

"Marian told me about what happened after that article in the paper came out. It made me sick just to imagine it. I can't even think about something happening to you."

At the counter Zach froze, his back to Leith.

Leith approached Zach slowly, wrapping his arms around him from behind and sighing when Zach melted against him. He kissed the side of Zach's neck. "I'm sorry that happened. I hate that I had anything to do with it."

"It wasn't your fault. Leith, you beat yourself up for enough at the time. Please don't do it again. I'm fine." He put his hand over Leith's on his chest. "I'm fine," he repeated.

Squeezing him tightly, Leith breathed in Zach's sweet-spicy scent. "Okay," he whispered. He sucked on the soft skin behind Zach's ear.

"So you went to the club."

"Yes. It...it felt good to be there. I'm just talking about a little training for now. It'll be good for me. Help with my aggression."

Zach was weak in Leith's arms. He shook his head. "I know you, Leith. It'll start with a little training, but you'll want more."

Leith turned Zach and kissed him softly before resting their foreheads together. He whispered, "I might, and if I do, I'll need your support. My fancy footwork isn't so fancy anymore, and my reflexes are slow. I doubt I could compete again anyway."

Zach sighed, his eyes big and intense. His hand came up to touch Leith's face. "You can do anything you set your mind to, and no matter what, I'll be there by your side." Zach eyes flashed then, and he banged gently against Leith's chest with his fists. "But you have to start out slow, and no pushing it beyond what the doctors say is okay, and you have to promise me that—"

Leith kissed him. "I promise," he murmured. "I promise." He ran his hands over Zach's ass. "Do you have to get back downstairs?"

"Not even a little bit."

"I want you to fuck me. I want to feel you inside me. I want...I want it all." Leith couldn't stop touching Zach. Couldn't stop kissing him.

With a groan, Zach tugged Leith toward their room.

In their bed, Leith gasped at the intense stretch and burn as Zach pushed the thick head of his cock into Leith's ass. Chills broke out over his body as he pressed down, his legs shaking on Zach's shoulders and sweat sliding down his forehead. Zach's fingers had felt big, but his cock felt huge, and Leith took shallow breaths, trying to ride out the pain.

Zach stroked a hand down Leith's thigh and whispered, "There now. A little more. Breathe. You're doing great. Leith, you feel so good."

Leith whimpered as Zach slid in deeper. It was intense, and it hurt, and yet it was somehow good. Leith's ass gripped and released Zach's cock in fluttering, involuntary spasms with every inch that Zach pushed in. Leith felt a flush rising up his body. His nipples tingled and he felt a strong urge to pinch them.

The sensations were overwhelming, and when Zach cocked his hips and thrust a little, Leith's entire body clenched and released with shock and pleasure, and he made a noise he'd never heard himself make before.

His own hands running over his chest and touching his nipples seemed to help ground him, and he held onto them as Zach pushed in with small, crazy-making thrusts. Leith squeezed his nipples when he felt the scratch of Zach's pubic hair against his ass and Zach's hard, thick length deep inside him.

The burn in his ass was offset by the look on Zach's face—pupils blown, and an expression of tender control. *Incredible.* Leith felt safe there with Zach's cock in his ass, somehow taken care of in a way he'd never known, and he relaxed, feeling Zach slide in the tiniest bit deeper.

"That's it, Leith," Zach whispered. "Just like that."

Leith squeezed his nipples again as Zach began to move, and he rolled his hips to meet Zach's thrusts. He froze as he was captured in insane pleasure, his mouth dropping open and a desperate sound coming from his throat. He knew he must have felt that breathtaking pleasure before, but he couldn't *remember* ever feeling anything like it. He whimpered, wanting to feel it again. Zach's smile was soft and a little amused, but he thrust harder, and Leith shuddered as Zach hit against his prostate again.

"Do you like that?" Zach asked.

Leith could see by his expression that Zach knew he did, so

he didn't answer, his eyes closing on Zach's next thrust. He might have left his body it was so good. He was lost in a rhythm of intense pleasure that left him shaking and nonverbal, grunts and moans coming endlessly from his open mouth.

He could barely catch his breath between the small, shivery, beautiful waves of intense bliss that consumed his entire body, like small orgasms that he was riding. It went on and on for what felt like hours, but at the same time only minutes, and he was utterly lost in it.

Zach's voice reached him from miles away with sweet words of affection. Leith wanted to show Zach the same amount of glorious ecstasy he was experiencing, but the feelings were just too much, and he clenched his nipples, seeking some grounding. But it only brought another small orgasmic wave, and he felt it rising, cresting, drawing out larger and larger, and he couldn't breathe. He was aching and wanting, and his cock felt so hard that it almost hurt.

He reached for it with one hand, and Zach met him there, pushing his hand away and taking Leith's cock in fast jerks that matched the rhythm of his hips. Leith didn't know if he could handle it. He was coming apart, and yet it was too good to want it to stop.

If he could speak he would have begged, but nothing came out of his mouth but wordless whimpers and grunts, and he realized he was lifting his hips to meet Zach, begging with his body. He pressed the heels of his palms against his eyes, trying not to explode with pleasure.

Then it happened without warning, He felt it first in his ass, and then his stomach, and then it rolled through his entire body, He jerked and shot a load of come so hard he felt the heat of it hit his own face, and he was swallowed in an orgasm like he'd never experienced before. Consuming and almost endless it held him in its grip.

As Zach lay on his chest, gasping and shuddering through his own orgasm, Leith ebbed out of the immense pleasure slowly, still whimpering. He wrapped Zach in his arms. Nothing compared to this. Not thousands of suns, a monsoon-swollen river, or even the unobservable universe.

ᕀ ᕀ ᕀ

It felt amazing to spar again.

He hadn't regained the strength he'd had before his injury, but while his reflexes were slower, his punches were still solid enough, and when he connected one to Marvin's chin, he leapt into the air. Leith wished Zach was there to see it.

Marvin rubbed his glove over his jaw. "You haven't lost it all, my friend. Good one. I think I need a break."

Leith grinned and used his teeth to rip off his glove after spitting out his mouth guard. "Thanks. It's awesome to be in the ring again. It's been a long time."

Marvin clapped Leith's shoulder with his taped hand. "You've still got it in you. You'll make a comeback yet."

Leith chuckled and shook his head, but he was hopeful as he headed for the showers. He stripped down and turned on the water, dunking his head under the stream and feeling the soothing coolness rush over him before the heat kicked in.

He remembered the day before with Zach. His ass still felt tender, and he'd been aware of it even when he was boxing. Being fucked had been amazing. He didn't even know how to process how much he'd liked it. It made him smile, and it made him break out in chills. It made him feel incredibly loved.

Thinking about the difference between how he felt when he was doing it to Zach and how he'd felt when Zach was doing it to him, he couldn't decide which emotion was sweeter. He loved feeling like he was protecting Zach, taking care of him, and he loved the sensation of Zach's ass around his cock. But he loved the way it felt to be fucked, which surprised and aroused him. He loved feeling safe enough to let Zach take care of him that way.

Leith realized that his dick was reacting to his thoughts, and he looked around, hoping that no one had noticed. He turned the water to cold, dousing his lust. Marian had told him how hard won his acceptance had been here, and he didn't want anyone to imagine he was getting turned on in the showers by any of them.

He toweled off quickly, eager to get back to Blue Flight to tell Zach how he'd done. He closed his eyes and imagined the smile Zach had given the old Leith in the photo in the paper. He hoped Zach looked something like that when he told him about the blow he'd landed on Marvin.

⤸ ⤸ ⤸

Zach did smile when Leith told him, and while it might not have been as blinding with pride, it was still a good smile. Leith sat at the bar, happy and content to watch Zach work. He chatted with Vanessa for a while, but then things got busy. He thought about helping, but instead enjoyed watching Zach rush around, totally in control of the situation.

A couple of guys came in holding hands, and Leith smiled. He hoped they were as in love as he was with Zach. When they sat next to him, Leith's contentedness fled almost immediately.

The younger one nodded toward Zach. "He's pretty hot."

Leith opened his mouth to say that Zach was also pretty taken.

But the other man said, "That one? Oh yeah, he's hot all right. And a hungry, eager little bitch."

Shaking, Leith clenched his fists. He heard a low growl starting in his throat.

"You've had him?" the smaller one seemed impressed.

"I sure did."

"When was this? And why wasn't I invited?"

"Eh, not too long ago. Last month or whenever it was you were away. It was good. I'd be up for it again, but maybe you want a shot at him? Or we could have him together. He seems like the type for that. You should hear the noises he makes. Begs for it—"

Leith didn't remember grabbing the guy and throwing him to the ground. He didn't remember punching him, or yelling, but he found himself being dragged away, Zach's hands clutching at him and his voice breaking through the fury.

"Leith! Leith, stop! Stop!"

There was some blood, but not as much as Leith wanted there to be. The guy on the floor looked terrified, his eyes wide and his mouth open with red dribbling from the side. Leith yanked at Zach's grip to leap on the man again, but Zach held on.

"Leith, please. *Please.*"

Some other guys held him back until he was pushed onto a stool at the bar, his heart pounding violently and his mouth wet with an urge to spit on the guy. It took everything in him not to lunge again when Zach grabbed the asshole's arm and helped him up. Trembling all over, Zach looked up at him with big pleading eyes—had he looked like that while the asshole *fucked* him?—and begged him not to file assault charges. *Begged* him.

Gagging, Leith wanted to rip Zach's hand away from the guy and punch the asshole again, his rage screaming through him. Sanity took hold long enough to force him to flee the scene, taking the stairs up to the apartment two at a time to put distance between himself and the object of his fury. Slamming through the apartment, his blood rushed in his ears as he made for the relative security of his bedroom.

His room was no help. The bed was still rumpled from the

175

sex they'd had that morning, and he ripped the sheets off and threw them on the floor. It wasn't enough, so he grabbed the closest thing he could lay his hands on and slammed it into the wall. The lamp shattered.

The new box of photos and letters he'd been looking through the night before was still open on his desk, and he grabbed a handful of pictures, his face twitching as he looked at the one on top of Zach laughing, his eyes bright.

"Leith?" Zach's voice was barely a whisper.

Leith whirled to face him in the doorway. "When were you planning on telling me you'd fucked someone else?" Leith threw the stack of photos at Zach's chest. They hit and scattered all over the floor in a splash of red, blue, green, black, and yellow.

Zach stood very still, looking as though he'd been slapped.

"Well?" Leith demanded.

"I wasn't going to tell you," Zach answered. "I didn't want you to know."

"That's great. That's just great." Leith shoved past him, slamming his fist into the punching bag. His knuckles stung from the blow. Leith turned back to Zach and sneered. "Well, now I do. And do you know what I think? This is what I think." Leith got in Zach's face and spat out the words, "Fuck you."

Zach's jaw clenched and he nodded slowly. "Okay," he said with slow and unusual deliberateness. "I made a mistake. I should have told you."

Leith snorted. "I thought I could trust you. I thought that I—you wouldn't believe what I thought, and all along you were just jerking me around, making an ass out of me."

"Leith—"

"Who knew about this? Everyone? Marian? Who?"

"Leith, it was one night. It was a mistake. I thought that—"

"You didn't tell me. You don't tell me *anything*. I don't even *know* you."

Zach lips trembled, but his eyes flashed. "You didn't need to know. There was no reason to tell you. He meant nothing to me—"

"Nothing! You fucked a guy who meant nothing to you? How could you do that? While I was in the hospital alone and fucked up you were out living it up? Fuck you. You've been lying all this time, and it's my life. It's *my* life we're talking about here."

"It was my life too," Zach snapped, stepping into Leith's personal space. "And you have no idea—"

"Yeah, well, it doesn't have to be anymore. You can go now. There's no need for you here." Leith grabbed a photo from the floor and forced it into Zach's hand. It was a photo booth picture of them kissing. "This? This is bullshit. This is nothing. I don't remember this and I never will."

Zach looked as if he was going to throw up, and Leith's throat felt tight, but he went on, "I don't need your sympathy, and I don't want your pity. You can stop feeling guilty about it and go get yourself fucked by someone else. I'm done with you."

Leith pushed past Zach and tried to slam the door behind him, but Zach caught it and thrust himself between Leith and his escape route.

"Leith!" Zach's voice seethed with anger. "I understand you're angry, but you're not the only person here who lost something that day."

"Oh yeah, like you lost so much."

"I lost *everything*," Zach screamed. His face twisted and his voice broke. "I lost the man I loved more than life, and he doesn't even *remember me*. He doesn't remember what we had, what we were, or how happy we were together. He doesn't remember the first time we made love, or the second, or the stupid fights we had that we thought were so fucking important.

He doesn't know how he used to look at me that made me feel like I would do, give, *be* anything if it was for him. He doesn't know that even now just being near him is the only thing I want—even now, even when he's disgusted with me—"

"I can't look at you."

Leith turned his back on Zach and unleashed on the punching bag in the corner, pounding it in rapid, hard bursts. Sweat slid down his back as he imagined the bag as the man in the bar, the disgusting bastard who'd talked about Zach like he was nothing, like he wasn't the most important thing in the universe, and thought about Zach opening himself for some other man and slammed with more force. Pain bloomed on his knuckles and he kept on, harder and harder.

"I'm sorry," Zach said, his voice barely audible over the smacks of Leith's bare fist hitting leather. "I made a huge mistake, and I should have told you. I would give anything to be able to take it back."

Leith didn't answer, focused entirely on pounding the bag until his hands broke or until the rage inside was exhausted.

"I have to deal with the bar now, Leith. I'll sleep tonight on the couch in the office down there until I can find a place to stay."

The door shut behind Zach, and Leith collapsed to the floor, burying his face in his hands. Hot tears burned like shards of glass and blank, hopeless terror pulsed through him as though it was something vicious and alive.

He didn't know who he was anymore or who he could trust. From deep down a cry pushed up and he wailed, "I want to go home!" His voice broke. "Just let me go home."

Night moved across the room slowly as he huddled in the corner. The sounds of cars occasionally vibrated the windows, adding texture to the darkness, and the rattle of the pipes gave vent to Leith's anxiety.

He stuffed a bag with some underwear, a change of clothes, the box of photos and letters, and a wad of cash. He didn't know where he was going, and he wasn't even sure he would actually leave. But sitting in the dark thinking of the pummeling he'd given the stranger in the bar, someone whose name he didn't even know—someone who'd had Zach—he didn't feel like he could stay either.

Leith took his cell phone from his pocket and turned it on. He typed in a text and discarded it without sending it. He noticed there was a forgotten draft already ready to send.

Zach, I don't understand it, but I think I'm in love with you.

After staring at the words for a long time, he deleted the message and sat the phone on the desk.

He wasn't sure where Marian and Ava were, and the door of the apartment shut behind him quietly. He walked down the stairs, hearing the soft echo on the walls. The city was drowsing, and though there were lights still on and cars moving all around, it was as though the world was at arm's length. It didn't take long for him to get a taxi, and from the backseat he watched the city disappear.

LATER THAT NIGHT
VLOG ENTRY #10

INT. LEITH AND ZACH'S BEDROOM
Still dressed in jeans and a rumpled shirt, Zach is slumped against the headboard of the bed. The computer is propped on something on the bed, and Zach reaches out to steady it several times. He doesn't look at the camera.

ZACH

Hello, my loves.

Things here have...imploded. Leith is gone. I don't know where he's gone to, and I don't know if he'll be back. He didn't leave a note. He just left.

He sighs and cups his hands under his chin.

We had a fight. Over that idiotic one night stand I had. The one I told you about. I never thought I'd see that guy again, and I never wanted to. It had been humiliating enough to live through, and I didn't want to be reminded of my mistake. But then he and his boyfriend showed up at Blue Flight. I don't know how Leith found out what happened, but he did, and all hell broke loose.

Zach shakes his head and fiddles with the bed clothes. He moves and nearly tips the computer over. He straightens it again.

The guy I slept with isn't going to press charges, and for that I'm grateful. Arthur talked to him, and for all I know he paid him off. The guy said he hoped things worked out for me and my boyfriend.

He rolls his eyes and throws up his hands.

I didn't even know what to say to that. He said he knew when we...well, he'd been able to tell that I was in a bad place in my life. He said he was drawn to that kind of thing; the desperation was a turn on for him.

He sighs.

I've been around enough to know what was going on when I put myself in that position, but hearing myself described through his eyes?

He picks at the hem of his jeans.

Leith didn't even know who I was! Everything we'd shared had vanished. It was all gone, and I just needed to feel something other than the black hole of despair. The worst part is that I let some asshole see my fear and desperation, and I never let Leith see that. Not even later when I should have. I couldn't. I was too afraid.

He looks at the long thread he's yanked free.

Unraveling. Yeah, that's about right.

He sighs and wraps the string around his finger.

I told myself that I was taking care of Leith, and if he saw how terrified I was, then he'd never trust me to take care of him. He needs me to be reliable, and he needs me to be the person he can turn to when he can't handle something for himself.

That's when I can see the weight lifted from his shoulders, and I feel stronger somehow, because I know I did that for him. But if he knew how confused I've been— how scared and sad? Where would that leave us? Who would shore up our sinking ship? I couldn't tell him what I'd done. There was already so much to deal with.

Zach's lips twist. He brings the finger with the string on it to his mouth, biting at the thread.

God! I'm an idiot. I've been going on and on about this stupid one night stand, and the bigger problem is that Leith has left, and I don't know where he's gone, or if he's coming back. I don't know what to do with myself. Arthur's worried, but he thinks Leith needs space to process things, and that he'll come back.

Zach unwinds the thread from his finger.

Arthur's right. He'll come back, and I need to be ready when he does. There's a lot to do around here, so I guess I'll sign off. I hope you're all enjoying the rollercoaster that is my life. If nothing else, I hope you're thinking to yourselves, Hey, at least my life isn't as bad as Zach's! At least my boyfriend or girlfriend still remembers who I am!

So, just remember kids, it could be worse. Cherish the good times.

Signing off.

Chapter Eleven

The driver was listening to an album of blues Leith didn't recognize, but struck him as classic and right for his escape from Brooklyn. The rhythm seemed to throb with the slide of the landscape out the window and the ache in his heart as Leith let himself drowse in and out of sleep.

A train to Penns Grove would have been faster and cheaper, but the taxi was private, dark, and lonely. Leith was in a rocking womb hurtling through darkness back to someplace older than he could ever dream of being, someplace that held memories he hadn't forgotten. A place that might clasp him tight, push his hair off his face, and kiss his cheek while murmuring that everything was going to be all right.

The old house was right where he'd left it. It was somehow a surprise to see it there, though of course it couldn't get up and walk away. It was small and brick, with a garden-lined path that was neater than Leith could remember it being since his mother had died. He paid the taxi driver and tucked what little money he had left back into his box of treasures.

He heard the taxi pull away and saw the vague shape of it drive off into the dawn light. He stood on the sidewalk outside the iron gate and stared up at the second window on the left. His bedroom had been the smallest room in the house, more of a closet really, but it had a window. So his mother had declared it a room, and she'd painted the walls blue just for Leith.

The room had been a surprise on his seventh birthday. There'd been a party that day, too, with some friends and streamers, and a birthday cake made with chocolate frosting and decorative sprinkles. His father had come home drunk and bitching about the expense of a party for such a little kid, and Leith had spent his first night in his own room listening to Arthur's pounding stereo and the shouts of his mother and father.

As daylight crested behind the house, making it glow as though it were on fire, Leith looked at the living room window and remembered the soft green sofa his mother would sit on. She'd knit, or fold laundry, or simply stare out the window and hum under her breath. Her voice had been warm and safe like cocoa on a cold night.

Thinking back now, she'd always seemed so sad. Leith had often crept up by her and knelt at her side, resting his cheek against her knee, just listening. He bit his lip, remembering the soft cloth of her skirt and how it had felt so cool against his hot face.

Leith wanted to go to the backyard and look across to the fields he'd run as a child, to see if he could find the spot where he'd first seen that golden-crowned kinglet. But he didn't belong here now. It was morning and the house would be waking soon. At best his presence would be tolerated and at worst he'd be accused of trespassing, but most of all he didn't want to interact with anyone. He felt that if he were to speak now, the words would break him open and he'd spill everywhere—a fount of grief, fear, and tears.

He started walking. The streets were familiar and his feet knew where to go. It didn't take long, and by the time Leith entered the shadows of the woods, the sun was an orange ball just over the horizon. In the forest it was still dim and cool, with dappled morning sunlight flickering on the dark, leaf-strewn ground.

The place he sought wasn't as far in as he'd remembered, though. He supposed it had been quite a walk for his child legs to carry him. As an adult it wasn't even three minutes off the road.

The ground was still clear, and there were remnants of a cooking fire. Leith crouched down and poked at the ashes with a stick. He wasn't surprised children still camped here, but it was so familiar he might turn around and see himself with Arthur pitching the tent, or hear his father's footsteps approaching from the road to give them final instructions and a strong goodnight hug.

"I'll see you in the morning," their father would say, handing them both an extra flashlight. *"I'll kiss your mother for you. Be smart, my boys. Stay safe."* For all his faults, in the early years their father had been more good than bad.

After their mother died and Arthur had left, Leith camped here alone. His father would come to tell him goodnight only if he was sober—only if Leith hadn't escaped to the woods to get away from the phone that rang endlessly with creditors wanting their money, or bookies who wanted the same, or the neighbor who'd decided Leith was her responsibility and always wanted to check in.

Sober nights were rare, and yet when Leith sat by the ashes and looked up at the gray-blue sky beyond the branches, he could almost feel his father there—almost hear his footsteps on the ground behind him. He felt that if he turned around, his father would be there with a flashlight and a grin. *"Good morning, my boy. Did you dream enough for both of us?"*

Leith whispered, "I didn't dream last night, Dad. I didn't even sleep."

He waited for an answer and heard nothing except the rustle of squirrels in the bushes and the twitter of birds waking up. Cold in his t-shirt and jeans, Leith fell back onto the earth, his head cradled by the dirt and his arms and legs spread out limp. The sky was deep and endless, and somewhere up there it turned into space, and space turned into the observable universe, and the observable universe turned into *we just don't know.*

Leith didn't know a lot of things. He didn't know if there were police knocking on the door of the apartment to take him in on assault charges. He didn't know if Zach had found him gone yet. He didn't know if he wanted Zach to be mad, or sad, or scared. He didn't know if he *wanted* Zach. Hell, he didn't even *know* Zach.

And yet there it was, that feeling he couldn't shake. It was like a pull against his skin, something constant and ever present, as though it was part of him down to his cells, an emotion strong and compelling and rooted without logic. It was something he could only name as love.

The day swam in and around him in slow hours spent sifting through memories and emotions he couldn't contain. Alone in the woods he felt tears slide down the side of his face and drop off to the ground below. He alternated opening his eyes to stare up into the well of blue and closing them, taking comfort in the shifting colors under the black of his lids.

He sorted through the box he'd brought with him, reading again a beautiful letter from Naomi. She had loved him, and she'd left him because she believed he loved Zach. He read the words his father had penned to him in prison on the card he'd kept on a shelf by his bunk long after Christmas had passed.

He touched the worn-out photos of his mother, and one of his father standing with him and Arthur, a rare day without a fight between them. Then in the very bottom of the box was a note written on a glossy page torn from a magazine.

"I'm off to the store and then to work. You looked too peaceful to wake. Sweet dreams. I love you." Zach's name was signed. Leith ran his fingers over the letters and wondered why he'd kept this. Was it the first time Zach had expressed his love? Was it something else? What had moved him to save this scrap of a note?

Leith sighed and put it all back in the box, flopping back on the ground again to stare at the sky and let it all soak down into his bones. After the day passed through pink morning, white noon, gold afternoon, and into an amber of twilight, Leith stood, dusted himself off, and ran a hand over his sun-burned face.

The walk into town seemed longer than the walk into the woods. He felt raw and vulnerable, and exhausted with sun exposure and dehydration. The café was one he'd been to as a kid, and when he walked in, he half expected to see the old guy named Paul behind the counter, his French accent blurring the edges of his word. But there was a young woman there instead, a blonde with brown eyes and a happy smile.

She looked familiar, and Leith recognized her as he sat at a table in the corner. They'd gone to school together. She'd dated his friend. And they'd played Seven Minutes in Heaven together when they were nine. Leith had felt her flat breasts and kissed her dry lips in Marcus Neimbaum's closet. Her name was Eliza, and she'd been his first love Jennifer Dunaway's best friend.

"You look like you could use a drink," Eliza said, putting a glass of water down on his table. "Wait a minute now—Leith Wenz? Is that really you?"

Leith tried to smile and nodded his head. If it wasn't for the water, he'd have been out the door the moment he knew who she was.

"Wow, it's been years. You—you look good. Tired, but good."

"Thank you," Leith said, turning his head away and looking out the window.

Eliza sat in the empty chair across from him. "Are you here alone?"

"Looks like it," Leith said, biting back a sharper reply.

"I've heard good things, Leith." Eliza leaned forward. "Aren't you a boxer now or something? My mother was telling me about it, how you came out and got a ton of media for it. How you were in some magazine kissing your boyfriend—"

"We broke up," Leith said, surprised to hear the words come out of his mouth. He wasn't even sure if they were true.

"Aw, that's too bad." Eliza brushed her hair out of her eyes and smiled.

"Yeah, it is," Leith whispered.

Eliza pressed her lips together and her eyes grew empathetic. "So, what can I get you to eat? Something filling? My father-in-law makes an excellent Firehouse Chili."

Leith wasn't hungry, but he knew that he should eat. He had never liked chili, but it seemed like too much trouble to consult the menu. "Sounds great," Leith said, hoping that after taking his order she'd go away.

Eliza stood up but didn't make a move to leave. She leaned against a chair and continued, "Yeah, Adrien and I got married last year and I started working here this fall. My father-in-law was never very good with the patrons, so he's mainly in the back now."

Leith nodded and smiled with tight lips. He couldn't have this conversation right now. He cleared his throat and managed to say, "Yeah," and closed his eyes in hoping she would take the hint.

"It's good to see you, Leith. After the…well, when you ended up in prison I was really worried about you. When my mom told me about your boxing career, it was a relief to know you'd turned your life around."

"Thank you." His throat felt tight, and he downed some water in several long gulps.

"I'll get your chili," Eliza said, and put her hand on his

shoulder. "And more water."

Leith nodded and looked out the window. The street was just the way he remembered it, houses that backed up to fields down the east side, and a row of small businesses congregating toward the west. The sun was setting now, and the sky behind the buildings looked smudged with purple and pink.

Eliza put another glass of water down on his table and left without a word, leaving Leith thankful and ashamed at his lack of social grace. She'd been a nice girl. He hoped she was happy with Adrien, who was, if he remembered, a tall guy with dark hair and thick glasses. He glanced at Eliza as she sorted menus and noticed that her breasts were far from the flat nubs he'd run his palms over.

He considered them for a moment, thinking of the fleshy weight of a woman's breasts in his hands. He didn't find it unarousing, and yet when he thought of Zach, with his hard, strong chest and his biceps that fit perfectly in Leith's hands, Leith was shot through with a pang of lust. He drank more water, and watched an old lady balance several bags as she walked down the street.

The Firehouse Chili was filling, and as he finished it Eliza sat down at his table again, her eyes searching his face.

"Are you sure you're okay?" she asked. "Do you need a ride? Or to call a friend?"

"No, thank you. I'm just…visiting."

Eliza nodded but didn't look as though she believed him. She put out her hand and touched the back of his. "You know, Leith, when we were teenagers, I always wished you could see past Jennifer."

"Jennifer? Wasn't she your friend?"

"Yes, and she never thought much of you."

Leith exhaled sharply. It shouldn't have stung after all these years, but it did.

"I did, though. I thought of you a lot back then." Eliza looked down at where her hand rested on his and pulled her fingers away, tucking her hand under the table. "I don't know why I'm telling you. I'm happily married and you're…gay, but I just wanted you to know that, for me, you were always the one who got away."

Leith remembered a flash of wings as the kinglet flit into the bush. "I don't know what to say. I'm flattered, but—"

"There's no need for a 'but.' This was a confession, I guess. I just wanted you to know."

"Okay," Leith said, slowly. "Thank you." He swallowed and tried to smile. "Given how things went down between me and Jennifer, maybe I would've been better off if I had been able to see past her."

Eliza chuckled. "Well, her red hair was rather blinding. I had a hard time seeing past it myself."

Leith sighed and smiled as he stood. "I should go."

Eliza touched his arm. "Listen, if this sadness you've got going on is about that guy you broke up with, just…how can I say this? Well, I guess just make sure you're not being blinded by something—red hair or I don't know. Whatever. Okay?"

Leith swallowed hard, and then used the rest of his money paying Eliza. He thanked her again and wished her joy in her recent marriage before stepping out into the cool dark of evening. As he walked out of the café several people were on their way in, and Eliza greeted them with a smile.

It took a while for Leith to find a phone, but he located one finally behind the supermarket where his mother had bought their groceries. He pulled the slip of paper with the number on it from his wallet and dialed. He slumped against the booth when the voice at the other end was who he wanted to reach.

"Hey, it's Leith. Will you come and pick me up?"

જ જ જ

"I asked Ava to wait in the car," Marian said, crossing over to the swings in the darkness and squeezing into the one next to Leith. "I wanted to talk with you alone." She tugged at a piece of her afro, pulling the hair taunt before it bounced back gently.

Leith kicked at the dirt and pushed himself back and forth a little. "Thanks for coming for me. You didn't have to do that."

Marian looked at him as though he'd lost his mind. "Yeah, I'm going to leave my friend stranded miles from home with no money. Leith, we were all freaking out. None of us knew where you'd gone. Arthur…Zach…they were both worried out of their minds."

Leith softly snorted. "I'm sure Arthur knew I'd turn up."

"Yes, he thought you took off to the woods, but that doesn't mean he wasn't pacing our living room all night debating whether he should try to file a missing person report. We were all pretty scared. You disappeared late with no note and no phone call. You didn't even take your cell phone. Anything could have happened to you."

"Marian, I can take care of myself. You didn't have to worry."

"Well, we *did.* Yeah, sure you can take care of yourself. You're just stranded that's all. Stranded in the middle of…where are we, exactly?" Marian asked, looking around. "I mean, I know where we are, but *where* are we?"

"Where I grew up." Leith looked around. "I played on this playground. I went to that school. That was the field I played football on, and got my ass kicked by a bully. It's why I started boxing. Well, that and my father wanted me to learn."

Marian sighed. "Leith, you could've left a note."

"Yeah, I could have, but I didn't want to."

"That was pretty selfish of you."

Leith glowered. He wanted to say something hurtful back, but he just clenched his teeth together and gripped the ropes of the swing tighter.

Kicking herself off into some shallow swings, Marian said, "Zach's a mess right now."

Leith went tense all over. There was a reason he hadn't called Zach. He wasn't ready to talk with him yet. "This isn't about him."

"Come on, Leith," Marian scoffed. "It's about him."

Leith said nothing and kicked his swing high into the air, feeling the rush of wind gliding past him. Marian hopped out of her swing and stood in front of him, forcing him to a sudden stop.

"I told you before that he was devastated after your injury."

"Yeah, so?"

"I didn't exaggerate. I don't think there are words for what he went through."

"I don't want to hear about this shit," Leith growled, stumbling a bit out of the swing. Marian's hand was surprisingly strong when she grabbed his arm.

"You've got to hear it, Leith, Imagine it. Take some time and really think it over, okay? In a very real way, you *died* that day. Sure, your heart kept beating, and you kept breathing, and God knows we're all grateful for that, especially Zach. But he lost his partner that day. His best friend—the man he loved." Marian was earnest and serious as she gazed up at him. "Do you understand that?"

Leith stared into her dark eyes, feeling their intensity burn into him. He took some shaking breaths before looking at the tree-lined horizon, seeking something there to hold him to the earth.

"Can you really blame him?" Marian went on. "For looking for solace in the wrong place? Just once, Leith. And that nearly wrecked him too. I saw him after it was over, and he was a mess. A total mess. I had to come visit you the next day instead of him because he could barely hold himself together."

"Good," Leith heard himself say in a hard, cruel voice, and he was surprised by it. He wasn't sure he even meant it.

"No, Leith. It's not good. He felt guilty, like he'd betrayed you, and you *couldn't even remember him*. Do you *understand*, Leith? Can you *imagine* it? Put yourself in his shoes. Can you truly blame him? He thought he was nothing to you. That all you'd had was dead. You have to understand."

"No, *you* have to understand. I'm at his mercy. He holds all the fucking cards. He knows everything about me and I don't know him at all. He *fucked* that guy. Who else? How many times? For all I know he's been fucking around on me even when I was...when I was the me before the accident."

"No, Leith. No. Zach's not like that. You have so much more power over him than you know."

"How do I know what Zach's like? How do I know what *you're* like?" Leith choked and covered his mouth with his hand. He closed his eyes, shutting out the sky, the grass, the trees, and Marian's sincere face.

Marian stroked down his arm and took hold of his hand, squeezing it as they stood there. "I'm your friend and some deep down part of you recognizes that because when you needed someone to come get you, you called me. Not Arthur, not Ava, and not even Zach. You trust me, Leith, and that's because I'm trustworthy. And I'm telling you, so is Zach."

"I invested everything in him," Leith whispered.

"And that trust wasn't misplaced. I promise you that, Leith. You aren't powerless here and you can believe in Zach."

Leith swallowed hard and bit his cheek to keep back his

emotions. He was tired and raw. He was more exposed than he'd ever felt before, as though everything that was important to him was out on the table for the world to see.

"Let's go home," Marian said. "Come on, Leith, it's time."

Nodding, Leith let her lead him to the car, where Ava waited with glistening eyes and a worried frown as she twisted a hunk of her blond hair around her finger.

Leith slept listlessly in the backseat of Ava's car, his head rolling awkwardly on the headrest. Trees and cars flashed by the window in a strange, surreal tempo that mixed in his dreams.

Tree, tree, tree, car, car, tree. His mother singing softly by a flowing river, and Zach splashing out of the water as his mother dissolved in front of him. Car, car, car, tree, tree, trees in a clump, car, his father slapping Arthur on the back and then laughing about something Leith couldn't hear, but his heart swelled at the joy on his father's face.

The whir of the tires, the rush of a truck beside them, and then tree, tree, tree, car, car, car, clump of trees, two cars, and Zach sitting by a campfire with his shirt off, looking at him with big, emotion-filled eyes. Leith woke with his cock half hard and his hands shaking.

Ava and Marian talked in low tones in the front, and Leith was thankful they left him alone for the most part. Drifting in and out of sleep, he woke fully only when he saw the lights of the high rises as they entered the city. He forced himself to sit up as far as he could without hitting his head on the low ceiling of the car.

They drove past the boxing club, and Leith clasped his fingers together, thinking of taped hands, the scent of sweat, and the satisfaction of a punch well-landed. Boxing was it for him, and he knew he'd always go back to it, though he had to accept that he'd never remember his finest hours.

He'd lost those for good, never to be recaptured, because as they drove the waking streets of the city, he accepted once and for all that he'd never box competitively again. He was too slow, and it was too dangerous. Life moved on, and he was caught up in it, no matter what Dr. Thakur had said about swimming against the current.

Sometimes it took divine courage to let go and end up in an ocean of the unknown.

Letting the car carry him onward, he closed his eyes and tried to relax his body. He thought of the sea—of water that stirred slowly deep below the surface and drove the currents that traveled the globe.

He understood the water's motion, felt it within himself, and while his conscious mind yearned for a narrative to cling to—something predictable like the endless rise and dip of waves visible on the surface—he was only comfortable when following the commands of the deep currents within him. And they all flowed back to Zach.

Opening the door to the apartment, he didn't know what he was going to say to Zach. But as it turned out, there was nothing to say. The apartment was still and silent, and when Leith stepped into his room, sensing Marian and Ava entering behind him, both measuring his reaction, he saw immediately what Zach had done.

"Where did he go?" Leith asked, his throat tight.

"To his sister's," Ava replied, her blue eyes wide with earnest empathy.

Leith bit his lip and turned his back to them, looking at the bare places where Zach's things had been. "He's gone? Just like that?"

"No, not *just like that*," Marian said, impatience bleeding into her tone. "He's been through a lot, and it's been mounting for a long time. It's taken a toll on him."

"Yeah," Leith whispered. "I get that."

"And he isn't gone," Ava said, taking hold of Leith's arm gently. "He's just at Maddie's right now because he didn't know if he should be here when you got back. You made it clear to Marian you didn't want to see him right now."

"He didn't move out?" Leith asked.

"Of course not. His things are just down the hall in his old room."

Leith nodded, feeling a crazy urge to stalk down the hall and grab everything and bring it back. He sat on his bed instead, his elbows on his knees, staring blankly ahead.

Not too long ago he'd been in prison, and now it was three years later and he was in love with a stranger. He'd lost his father—and his mother all over again. There were two other strangers standing his room, looking at him with affection and love, and he didn't know what the fuck to do about any of it.

The glance exchanged between Ava and Marian made Leith nervous. "What?" he asked. "What aren't you telling me?"

Ava's face pinked. "Well, we didn't know if we should...I'm not sure we're even supposed to know about it, but... Sit at your desk. We want to show you something on your computer."

Leith didn't know if he wanted to see whatever they had to show him. They both seemed anxious, and suddenly Leith's mind was filled with crazy ideas and he wondered if they were going to show him some kind of porn Zach had starred in. His stomach clenched into knots and he felt like he might throw up.

"It's nothing bad, Leith." Ava gave him a smile. "I promise."

"It's just something that might help you understand Zach a bit better." Marian took his hand and pulled him up from the bed.

Leith allowed himself to be maneuvered into his desk chair.

He sat there, his heart racing and his gut twisting.

Ava leaned over and typed something into the address bar. "Oh, he made a new one after you ran off. But you need to start at the beginning. Here, let me show you…"

Chapter Twelve

The room was quiet now except for the sound of the computer fan whirring, and the shuffling and banging of the girls making a late snack in the kitchen. They'd left at some point during the first vlog entry, but Leith wasn't sure when. He'd been glued to the screen, his heart in his throat.

As Leith had watched Zach and heard the anguish in his voice, the powerful undercurrents he'd felt driving him for weeks rose to the surface and crashed onto the shore of his consciousness. Tears had streamed down his face as he'd watched each gut-wrenching entry.

Now as he sat staring at a screensaver showing the curl of an ocean wave with a tiny surfer emerging, he flashed on the moment he first saw Zach in the doorway to his hospital room and he'd remembered the golden-crowned kinglet, broken and wounded.

He remembered Zach by the lake at the cabin, alone and despondent, setting his shoulders with determination before returning to the house. There had been so many moments after that—sweet sparks of vulnerability that Leith reacted to instinctively by wanting to touch and hold Zach.

There were three things he knew for certain now. He loved Zach beyond reason, he could trust Zach with his heart and soul, and Zach needed him more than he needed Zach. It was the last one that came as the biggest surprise, though he didn't know why. The first two fed so hungrily on the last that it seemed completely obvious now.

He clicked on the first vlog of them together, watching it for the sixth or seventh time. Leith was not the person in the video, not anymore. It wasn't only that he didn't remember the life that the old him had led, but Leith could tell that the person in the vlog didn't know how much Zach needed him, and instead only knew how much he needed Zach. That Leith had never been so lucky as to know what Leith now saw so clearly.

Leith paused the first video during a kiss, studying the screen thoughtfully and feeling nothing more than a strange happiness that he wasn't that guy anymore. "Leith?" Zach's voice was quiet from the doorway, where he stood with one arm over his chest.

His red eyes and solemn expression made Leith want to drag him into his arms and kiss the sorrow away.

"Can I come in?" Zach asked.

Leith nodded as he stood, tucking his hands into his pockets to keep from touching Zach too soon.

"Marian and Ava called to let me know you were okay. I was going to stay away, but—" His voice cracked. "I needed to talk to you. Leith, I'm sorry. I should have told you. I made a mistake—"

"Yeah, you did make a mistake," Leith interrupted. "You should have trusted me. You should have told me how you felt, instead of talking to strangers on the internet. You should have told me everything from the beginning, from the very first day. You should have *insisted* on me being told the truth about us and not insisted that they hide it. So yeah, I'd say you made some pretty big mistakes."

Zach swallowed hard and shut the door behind him. He nodded, apparently accepting Leith's words without defense or argument.

"And you shouldn't have moved your stuff out of here. Now we'll have to move it all back, which is a waste of time that we could have spent doing something else."

Zach's forehead creased. "What?"

"We could have spent that time talking or..." Leith walked to Zach and put his arms on his shoulders, leaning down to whisper in his ear. "Making up."

Leith pulled him close, his heart racing. His stomach curled into a knot as he breathed in the smell of Zach's cologne, sweet, spicy, and so achingly familiar. Zach's hair felt soft against his cheek, and his breath was hot and coming in hard gasps against Leith's neck. The incredibly still way he stood in Leith's arms gave away how very desperately he wanted to make the hug last.

Leith shuddered and leaned back to look into Zach's eyes, the green-blue fringed with feathery lashes, shining with terror and hope. Zach's mouth was soft and tremulous, and Leith swallowed hard. He couldn't resist. Zach's mouth was so hot and wet—so right. Leith's knees almost buckled as he twisted his fists into Zach's shirt, pulling him closer.

Zach's hands went to his face and his hair, pulling him in for more every time Leith broke for a breath. Leith pushed Zach against the wall, holding him there with his body. God, he needed more. Zach's t-shirt was in the way now, so Leith found his way way under the hem, pushing it up to run his fingers over hard muscle and soft skin.

"Leith," Zach gasped. "Let's just—Leith—"

Leith didn't want to *just* anything. He wanted to keep kissing, to touch and smell Zach, to grab handfuls of his hair and shove against him until he collapsed in orgasm and the crazy feeling that overwhelmed him—the thing that was like happiness and comfort and want and need and God-so-good all in one—made them both feel whole again.

Leith couldn't speak. He could only kiss and moan, and Zach had his hand right where Leith needed it now, Leith's jeans shoved down as Zach jerked him the way he liked it, firm and rhythmic. Leith tried to get his hand between them to touch Zach, but Zach just pushed it away. Leith would have been frustrated except he could feel Zach's hips thrusting against his thigh, and Zach's eyes were big and hot, and incredibly focused on him. Leith kissed him again, sucking Zach's bottom lip.

Leith whimpered and pressed their foreheads together. "Zach," he choked out as he shuddered and rocked in Zach's hand. He was so close, so close, and Zach was watching him now with such tenderness. Leith slammed into orgasm, his hips jerking uncontrollably, his vision graying out, and soft wild sounds coming from his throat.

He collapsed a little, letting Zach's strength hold him up. He was shaking and spent. Somewhere deep in his mind he knew that from now on, no matter what, raging wouldn't do any good. Fighting the past wouldn't help either, but he didn't have to freak out, because he'd done that already and this is where he'd end up again.

"Zach—" Leith whispered.

"Shh," Zach said, smoothing his hand through Leith's hair and clasping the back of his neck. "Just...shh."

"I love you."

Zach trembled. "I know. I love you too. I'm sorry for what happened."

Leith ducked his head, ashamed. "No, I'm sorry. I...I scared myself and I know I scared you."

"Leith, you were triggered."

"I should have more control. It's just the things he was saying about you—I saw red. Can I claim brain damage?"

Zach chuckled and shook his head. "You could, but do you really want to?"

"I'm so sorry, Zach."

"I know. Leith...you have to know that he meant nothing. I

was lost without you and I did something incredibly stupid. I didn't know if you'd ever...if we'd... I was so fucking afraid."

Leith closed his eyes and held Zach tight, fighting off the image of Zach going to a stranger to be taken care of and have his fear eased. He caressed Zach's cheek. "Zach, from now on I want to know everything. I want you to tell me about who I was before, and I want you to tell *me* about missing him, not some random people online. *I* want to know everything about you."

Zach lips trembled but he nodded.

"I already know your secret, Zach. You're lost, and you think I won't want you if I know that. You're wrong." He forced Zach's chin up, looking into his eyes. "I need you. I love you and I'm not going anywhere."

"Same here," Zach whispered.

"I know," Leith murmured against Zach's lips before kissing him.

The bed was the only place Leith wanted to be. As they moved there together they left their clothes on the floor. Hot, needful seconds turned into desperate, wanting minutes. Splayed on his back under Zach's mouth, hands, and body, Leith didn't know if Zach was torturing him or making love to him. He was strung out near orgasm and his cock ached but Zach wouldn't let him touch it, pushing his hands away and holding them down.

"Only when I say," Zach whispered.

Sweat broke out all over his body as Zach slid his hand between Leith's ass cheeks and rubbed fingers against his asshole, testing the lube he'd applied when he'd rolled on the condom a few minutes earlier. The circling fingers brought up a sweet aching feeling that made Leith twitch his hips and turn his face into the pillow, a non-verbal plea for Zach to go on.

Zach's middle finger slid in pretty easily, and Leith felt his ass clenching around it. The next finger wasn't as painless, but

Leith didn't care. He couldn't stop kissing Zach. The fingers in his ass burned some, but that just made him feel hot everywhere. He breathed in and out with staccato, shaking breaths as Zach finger fucked him.

It went on and on, and when Leith moaned for more, Zach shushed him and continued to play with his ass. Leith could barely keep his eyes open. The sensations cascading over him were making him crazy, and he whimpered eagerly when Zach finally lifted his legs onto his shoulders.

Zach's cock against his asshole was thick, and the tight, burning stretch pulled a moan from Leith. One of Zach's hands moved to his hip, holding him steady as the other gripped his leg tightly. The sweet slide after Zach's cockhead passed the tight ring of his anus was so incredible that Leith slammed his hips up fast, needing more.

Zach grunted and bit his lower lip, his eyes hot. "Easy, Leith," Zach murmured.

Swallowing hard, Leith met Zach's thrusts, riding the crazy shivery waves that rushed over him with every brush against his prostate. "Zach, please," Leith murmured, and Zach bent to kiss him, licking into his mouth and kissing down his neck. Leith grabbed his own nipples and squeezed, his toes curling and uncurling, and his cock dribbling pre-come.

"Zach, please. I need to come."

"Soon."

"Now." Leith reached for his cock.

Zach smiled and pushed Leith's hands away again. He held them down on the bed and rode him harder and faster. Aching, Leith closed his eyes and let go. It was too good, oh God, too good. He couldn't deal with it for much longer and he was shaking, trembling like a leaf. His heart pounded so hard it thrummed in his ears.

"Zach, please. Zach, ah, God…"

He was breathless now, his cock slapping against his stomach again and again. It was almost enough to make that final push into orgasm, but he just couldn't reach it. Zach's voice was layered over everything, but he couldn't make out words anymore. He was shivering and shaking, pushing his hips up to meet Zach's thrusts.

He tossed his head on the pillow, sweat slid down his face, and his ass clenched in spontaneous rhythm around Zach's cock. Suddenly he flew apart. The bed and Zach and his own body disappeared in a breathless endless moment. Then he was slammed back into coming and coming and coming, his hands clenched in the sheets, his body arched up and reaching, his cock issuing thick, white streams of come.

He was loud too. He couldn't keep quiet as it went on and on, leaving him trembling and weak, whimpering as the orgasm slowly ebbed with small shuddering contractions.

Zach pulled out of his ass, and Leith moaned in disappointment, wanting more even though he was exhausted and covered in come. Zach pulled the condom off and started jerking his own cock, his eyes raking over Leith's body eagerly. Leith watched, trying to catch his breath, as Zach's eyes closed, his face crumpled, and he shot a hot load onto Leith's stomach.

The noises Zach made were amazing. Leith shuddered through another aftershock before pulling Zach down to him and their beautiful mess, kissing and rubbing his back.

"Was that good?" Zach asked.

Leith scoffed softly. He held Zach even closer and kissed the soft skin of his neck. He wanted to know how the old Leith had met Zach, but he waited to ask, not wanting to mar the moment. He knew that for Zach, it was the beginning of the story that ended with losing his lover—the one who'd died when Leith lost his memories. He kissed Zach's neck again, tightening his arms around him and willing him to feel how much he loved him.

"Well?" Zach asked again, squirming in Leith's arms and smearing their sticky come between them.

Leith grabbed Zach's hips, holding him still, and whispered, "I don't know. You'll have to show me again later so I can be sure."

Zach smiled and kissed Leith's neck. "I think I can manage that."

"I'm going to shower." Leith didn't move a muscle.

"I can probably manage it in the shower even."

Leith chuckled. "You might have to manage it alone."

"Now, *that* I might have some trouble with."

"Good thing you have me."

Zach brushed their noses together. "Good thing we have each other."

Leith kissed him through the swell of emotion that crested over him. Then he laughed and flipped Zach before jumping up and grabbing a towel from the hook on the back of the door. "First!" Leith yelled, darting out the door with Zach scrambling to get his boxers on to catch up.

FOUR MONTHS LATER
VLOG ENTRY #11

INT. BLUE FLIGHT – BOOTH – NIGHT
Zach sits next to Leith. He's smiling and tapping his fingers on the table, while Leith relaxes next to him, slumped down in the booth, eating bites of cheese. Zach salutes the camera.

ZACH
Hello, my loves. It's been over four months since my last confession.

LEITH
Yeah, for all these months people have been emailing, wondering if I ever came back or if I was on the missing persons list.

ZACH
He claps his hand over Leith's mouth.

As you can see, Leith came back!

LEITH
Prying off Zach's hand.

Over four months ago, for the record. I was gone for, like, a day and a half.

ZACH
Yes, well. Ahem. Shhhh, this is my vlog, remember? So, my loves, he returned and we worked things out. We are now one hundred percent on the same page. About everything.

LEITH
He scoffs.

Oh yes, we are so simpatico that our hearts beat in sync. I never want to spank his bossy ass, and he never calls me a stubborn jerk, and we never argue. Ever. Oh, except for the fact that it's exactly the opposite of that. Especially the part about him being bossy.

ZACH

Leith is too modest. He doesn't want anyone to get any ideas about how amazing being with me is, or someone might show up and try to steal me away from him.

LEITH

He lifts his chin and narrows his eyes at the camera.

Just try it. I'll take you down.

ZACH

And he would. But hey, enough of that. Let's catch up on our lives. Leith is doing well, as you can see. He's finished his outpatient treatment, and even though he won't admit it, he misses his flaky doctor. Leith uses a lot of water metaphors now and talks about exploring the universe. It's all very deep.

He ignores Leith's glare.

He's also boxing sometimes, but has decided— thank God— not to try to do it competitively. He's working a bit at Blue Flight, but the best thing is he's started back to school. He's majoring in psychology, actually.

LEITH

He chuckles.

LEITH (*cont'd*)
Yep. That about sums it up.

ZACH
And I'm still busy as ever at the bar. Blue Flight was written up recently as the fifteenth most hip place to be in all of Brooklyn.

LEITH
Fifteenth most hip. That's one better than sixteenth.

ZACH

Zach punches him in the chest and Leith moans and plays it up.

Can it, smart guy.

Leith makes a motion with his hand to zip his lips. Zach kisses him quickly before turning back to the camera.

Now, what was I saying? Oh, right! Things are good here.

LEITH
Great even.

ZACH
Now who's bragging?

Leith points at himself with wide eyes and mouths silently, "Me? Bragging? What?"

But it's true, my lovelies. Things *are* great here, and I'm only sorry that I took so long to report it to you. I'll try to do better. I vow to update this every week—

LEITH

Unless his boyfriend forgets him again, and then he might be too depressed to update for a while.

ZACH

He laughs.

Babe, come on. Don't even joke. But, yes, if Leith breaks his promise to never forget me again—

LEITH

Not going to happen. I never break promises.

ZACH

Maybe we should knock on wood.

They both rap their knuckles on the table.

LEITH

Seriously, I won't forget you, though. I have a very good memory for an amnesiac.

So yes, before this gets any more ridiculous, we'll say goodbye.

He waves to the camera.

See you next week! *Mwah*!

Bye!

He turns to Zach.

Wait, who are you?

ZACH

Shut up. I love you.

LEITH

I love you too. It's...Rick, right? No wait, don't tell me. Zeke? Am I getting warmer?

ZACH

You're triggering PTSD in me, asshole.

LEITH

He grins.

Let me kiss it better.

The End

Author's Notes

First, I'd like to apologize for the oversimplification of amnesia and brain trauma. I did a lot of research into both, but in the end decided that the purpose of this story was to have fun exploring the well-worn romance cliché of amnesia and the romance of falling in love all over again. For that reason I downplayed the reality of the medical side of things, and I hope you're able to suspend disbelief to enjoy the story.

Second, I'd like to thank all of the amazing readers out there who have read and enjoyed my other books—inspiring me, supporting me, and generally making my dreams of being an author come true. No book is complete without a reader, and all of you hold a dear place in my heart. Thank you!

Thank you to inspiration in unexpected places. Thank you to Eknath Easwaran and Carole L. Flinders, especially.

Thank you to my beta readers for their excellent help: Jed, Cindy, Keira, and Indra. And thank you to Tracy and Beth for reading through very early versions.

Thank you to Keira Andrews for a wonderful, amazing editing job and for her dedicated friendship.

Thank you to Jed, Kim, Liza, Rachel, and Jacyn for years of friendship and love.

Thank you to my parents and in-laws for absolutely everything. And thank you to my daughter for being so understanding when imaginary people demand Mommy's attention. Thank you to my husband for his love, faith, and unfailing encouragement.

All my best,
Leta Blake

About the Author

While Leta Blake would love to tell you that writing transports her to worlds of magic and wonder and then safely returns her to a home of sparkling cleanliness and carefully folded laundry, the reality is a bit different. Instead, piles of laundry and forgotten appointments haunt her life, but the joy of writing and the thrill of finishing a book make the everyday chaos all worth it.

Leta's educational and professional background is in psychology and finance, respectively, but her passion has always been in writing, and she most enjoys crafting romance stories that she would like to read. At her home in the Southern U.S., Leta works hard at achieving balance between her day job, her writing, and her family.

You can find out more about her by following her at the following places:

letablake.wordpress.com

facebook.com/letablake

twitter/letablake

Other Books by Leta Blake

Training Season

Free Read
Stalking Dreams

Tempting Tales with Keira Andrews
Earthly Desires
Ascending Hearts
Love's Nest

Manufactured by Amazon.ca
Bolton, ON

13574663R00118